# * Brief Encounter *

A well-bred lady should swoon at such treatment, Felicia thought wildly. If she swooned, however, it would not be from outrage, but because the feelings going through her had turned her knees to jelly while rockets seemed to be going off within her head. Every nerve seemed to carry the fiery message his lips were imprinting upon hers, until she felt she must burst into flame.

When he finally broke off the kiss, she felt as if she had been spun about in a whirligig. The hands she had put up in an attempt to push him away were scrabbling at the front of his waistcoat, as much to support herself as in an attempt to embrace him, while his lips left hers to wander about her face and throat.

She uttered a sound midway between a sigh and a moan as his teeth caught her earlobe, nipping it gently. His breath was warm, stirring her hair, as he whispered, "And shall I show you what else happens to little girls who come to a man's bedroom?"

# A Husband for Holly

## Monette Cummings

CHARTER/DIAMOND BOOKS, NEW YORK

A HUSBAND FOR HOLLY

A Charter/Diamond Book / published by arrangement with
the author

PRINTING HISTORY
Charter/Diamond edition / October 1990

ISBN: 1-55773-400-3

Charter/Diamond Books are published by The Berkley Publishing
Group, 200 Madison Avenue, New York, New York 10016.
The name "CHARTER/DIAMOND" and its logo are trademarks
belonging to Charter Communications, Inc.

PRINTED IN THE UNITED STATES OF AMERICA

10  9  8  7  6  5  4  3  2  1

# A Husband For Holly

# * One *

"YOU ARE NOT Lady Felicia Arsdale, and I can prove it."

Felicia stared at the angry young man who was standing on the far side of her desk. Clad in worn buckskins and a leather waistcoat, and with his shirt open at the throat, he resembled a farm worker. Or a pirate.

What was he doing in her home? Hastings, her butler who customarily knew everything that went on in the house, had not announced him. Had he somehow managed to slip into the building unseen by the butler as well as the footmen, and what reason had he for being here?

She had been seated at the rosewood desk. From time to time she would stop her task to admire its inlay of butterflies made of some darker wood and mother of pearl, its top almost covered with the many invitations she and Holly had received in the past several days. As she reread each invitation and made an attempt to decide which of the more interesting ones would do them the greatest good, he had suddenly appeared before her, making his preposterous denunciation.

With his arms folded across his chest, he stood looking down at her so accusingly that she thought he must truly have divined her deception as he claimed to have done. But how could he, or anyone, have done that? She had been so careful in all the plans she had made.

Automatically, she put up a hand to touch the gray wig which had, until now, successfully convinced everyone that she was a middle-aged lady. She had a feeling that those sharp eyes had seen through her disguise.

"But I have never claimed that I am Lady Felicia," she protested, wondering why she was even deigning to reply. This man was, after all, a total stranger, someone who had made his way surreptitiously into her home.

She was the legal tenant of this house, and whatever she might do—here or elsewhere—was certainly none of his affair. Yet there was something in the stern look of those brilliantly blue eyes that was compelling her to answer him.

A raised eyebrow showed his disbelief of her statement and she said more forcefully, "I have never made any claim whatsoever to being Lady Felicia. In fact, whenever anyone has made that error, I have always taken the greatest pains to deny it."

"Then I must doubt that you have ever actually denied it sincerely enough to have anyone believe you. For it is clear enough that, whoever you really are, you are not who you pretend to be."

"That is not so. I—"

The young man—by his slyness in entering her house without being detected and the arrogance with which he faced her as he made his charge against her, she could scarcely think of him as a gentleman—stepped around the desk to her side.

Before she could move away from him, he hooked one finger beneath her wig and pulled forward a strand of brown hair. Twisting it about his finger, he said, "It is quite careless of you, my girl. You should have added several wrinkles if you planned to gammon the *ton*. I think this is quite enough to prove your deception. Now, exactly who are you?"

In another instant, she told herself, she would call

Hastings and have him summon several strong footmen to throw this obnoxious creature into the street. Or have him taken in charge, if that was the proper term, for making his way into her house uninvited. She could not understand why she had not already done so, or why she felt she must give him an answer.

"I do not know how you come into this house, who you are, or what affair you think any of this may be of yours, but I *am* Felicia Arsdale."

"Do not lie again."

"Not Lady Felicia, of course—I have always said that I am not her ladyship—but it happens that I am a distant connection of hers, although we have never met. And there is nothing you can do to prove that I am not who I claim to be, for I am telling the truth."

"But how many do you think will believe you, if I talk—if I tell everyone that you are attempting to gammon the *ton* into accepting an adventuress?"

"Adventuress!" She was on her feet at that, sending glances which should have slain him, but his additional size still gave him an advantage. He was almost six feet tall, at least half a head taller than she, and he towered over her, menacing her by the width of his shoulders as well as by his height.

"Is that not what everyone would call her if they knew the truth?"

Felicia knew he was right. He could ruin her carefully laid plans for Holly if he could convince her new friends that she was truly no more than she had told everyone she was.

Even during her short stay in London, she had learned that the scandal-loving members of the *ton* would be only too eager to take up such a tale and pass it along with their own embellishments. Ignoring the fact she had told them no more than the truth—at least, the truth about her name, if not about her age—from the day she had arrived in the city, they would be only too quick to convince themselves that Felicia Arsdale was an imposter who was trying to foist off an unknown girl upon the *ton*.

If he thought that he could frighten her by making such threats, he was right. She *was* frightened, not for herself, but because of what his threats could do to her plans for her sister. However, he was much mistaken if he thought she would show her fear of him by so much as the blink of an eyelash.

Felicia thrust out her chin, telling him in icy tones, "If you are planning to blackmail me, it will not work. I have done nothing wrong. And I am not wealthy, so I cannot pay blackmail. You must think again."

"Oh, I was not thinking of asking you for money," the stranger replied. "What I had in mind was more of a trade."

His blue eyes gleamed and his full lips curved into a smile as he said the last words. Had she met him elsewhere than here, she might have thought that his smile was quite charming. Doubtless, he was in the habit of using it, along with his pleasantly deep voice, to persuade people, especially females, to whatever purpose he had in mind.

At the present time, however, coupled with the threats he had been making, the smile repelled her, rather than attracting her. She had far too great a stake in this venture to succumb to blandishments from this or any other man.

"A trade?" Her own voice was full of suspicion.

"Yes. Your silence for mine."

"My silence? About what?"

"About me, of course—Auntie."

"But I know nothing whatsoever about you, so what could I say?" she demanded. "At least, there is nothing against you that I could prove. Even if you have made your way into my home uninvited, I do not suppose there is any way that I can have you taken in charge as a housebreaker.

You no doubt have some way of proving that you were invited in. Although I should like very much to—" At that moment, his last word penetrated her anger. "And do not call me 'Auntie!'"

"Ah, but that is what you will be to all the world. That is my second condition. I am not known to the *ton*, of course, and that is a state of affairs I find it necessary to change."

"I doubt anyone whom I know will care in the least to make your acquaintance, so your efforts to become known will be quite wasted. The people whom I meet are ladies and gentlemen." She kept her voice as cool as his, although it was an effort to do so, aware that he would have an advantage if she shouted at him as she would have liked to do.

"Those are the ones I wish to meet. And they will not object to me when they see my excellent credentials. You are to present me to them as your nephew—and everyone will suppose, of course, that I am the nephew of the real Lady Felicia."

The man was quite daft; that was the answer. She must not antagonize him, lest he become violent. If only there was some way that she could summon the servants to her aid without rousing his suspicions. "I see. But have you thought—whoever you are—"

"Oh, did I neglect to introduce myself? That was quite remiss of me." He bowed deeply. "Trevor Thomas—at your service, Auntie."

"I have told you not to call me that." Despite her feeling that it would be safer for her to remain calm, her indignation was growing with every word she heard and with every attempt on his part to ingratiate himself with her. Growing to the point that she finally cast all caution to the wind and reminded him, "And while you are being so clever with your scheming, you must have forgot—Lady Felicia *has* no nephew. If she had, he would be the new earl."

"Wrong again, Auntie. There are nephews and nephews, you must realize. I shall be related on her mother's side of the family, so no one will see anything amiss in the relationship." He grinned as if he felt he had gained another point in their contest.

"You are the most complete scoundrel I have ever seen," Felicia told him in disgust. "And if you think for one moment that I would involve myself or my niece in such a deception—"

"Is it any worse than your present one?" he said softly, but with menace.

"Certainly. I have done nothing to deceive anyone, as I have told everyone that I am *not* Lady Felicia." She repeated her earlier words with an air of triumph which he destroyed immediately.

"But you did not say it convincingly enough. You *wished* them to be deceived, even if you have been telling yourself that you did not. Therefore, even if your name is Felicia Arsdale—and I must doubt such a tale—if I were to offer proof that you are not the Lady Felicia everyone believes you to be, you know that you would find yourself—and your niece, if that is who she is—in disgrace."

She *had* told everyone the truth—to a point—so how could he have proof to offer of any deception on her part? At least, about her name. But what if he was able to concoct some sort of tale which he could persuade people to believe?

Nothing was more fragile than a reputation. And if she were discovered to be an imposter—and she was one in a way, she supposed, even if not in the way that he meant—she would have ruined all of Holly's chances for a brilliant marriage.

Had she no one but herself to consider, she would have told him to do his worst. But there was Holly's future to keep in mind and nothing must be allowed to endanger that. Its success was far too important to be jeopardized.

"Very well," she conceded, since she could see no way out of this coil. "I shall introduce you as you wish." She turned back to her desk, unwilling to face the look of triumph he must be wearing.

"I thought you would see my side of the matter. And now, for my third condition—"

"There is nothing more I can do for you, for which I am quite thankful."

"Yes, there is one more condition, only a small one, this time, I assure you." She thought he actually seemed to be purring with satisfaction at having gained those points so easily. Doubtless that gave him the reprehensibility to demand another. "Everyone would think it odd, if not quite scandalous, if I were to permit two ladies of my family to live here without giving them my protection."

Felicia swung about to stare at him. "You cannot mean—not even you would—"

"Ah, but I do mean. And I certainly would. Before nightfall, I shall have my things moved into the house. You will see how much more convenient that will be to have me here."

"Convenient? It would be nothing of the kind." It would be most dangerous to have him so near, whether he was a madman or the scoundrel she had called him. "Rather, it is a most improper suggestion. You are a stranger—"

"To you, I own that I am. But that is a condition that will not last for long. You will soon come to know me. And to the *ton*, I shall be your most dutiful nephew, Trevor. That is how you will introduce me."

"But not even a nephew would make his home with two unattached ladies."

"Perhaps it would be frowned upon if you were both young females. However, you have gone to much trouble to

convince everyone that you are a middle-aged aunt."
Again, he wrapped the strand of brown hair about his
finger, then tucked it out of sight beneath the wig, chuckling
when she shuddered at his touch.

"You have done it quite effectively, I may say, although
I still think some added wrinkles would have been a good
idea. So, rather than being shocked by my being here, the
*ton* will merely think I am being kind to my dear aunt, when
I offer you my escort and—as I have already said—my
protection."

Felicia scowled and started another protest, but his voice
hardened. "Understand this, my dear 'Auntie.' I do not trust
you out of my sight. Until both our aims are achieved—the
marriage of your beautiful niece, and my establishment as a
member of the *ton*—I shall go everywhere that you go. You
may be a trickster, but you will find that you have met your
match."

For several moments, Felicia stared at him in stunned
silence, then found her voice. "This is outrageous. I
absolutely refuse—"

"Please yourself, my lady. Either I move into the house
and you introduce me to the *ton* as your nephew, or I shall
spoil your pretty scheme. Perhaps you think I do not have
the proof I mentioned, but dare you take that chance?"

He knew she did not dare. Still she protested, "But—but
I cannot allow you to come here. Holly would know that we
are not related."

"That pretty shatterbrain you have been presenting as
your niece? You certainly can spin a tale that she would
believe."

Felicia fumed. "Pretty shatterbrain" indeed! She might
own to herself that Holly was a widgeon, but what right had
this creature to disparage her? And pretty was much too
mild a term to apply to such an Incomparable as Holly.

"And how do you expect to make Holly believe that you

are her brother?" Her tone was scathing, but he only laughed.

"Not her brother, of course, but her cousin. Both of us sponsored for the Season by our dear Aunt Felicia. She should believe that."

"Why should you wish a sponsor?" With his arrogance, the man could make his way anywhere; certainly he did not need her help.

"As I told you, no one knows me, so I should not receive any invitations of note. It would be a difficult task to establish myself in only a single Season. But as the nephew of Lady Felicia Arsdale, I would be welcomed anywhere."

So that was it—he was in London in search of a wealthy wife. She was certain he was not the only man in the city who had that goal in mind, although there were few who would take so wild a way of obtaining their objectives. When he found a wife, surely they would be free of him. There was hope that she would not find herself burdened with him for long.

"I—I suppose I could tell Holly *something*. As you say, she might accept that you are a cousin."

"Good girl." The scoundrel actually patted her cheek! "I shall bring my things at once."

"And I suppose you expect me to foot your bills, as well? You may as well know at the outset that I cannot afford to do so. We are not wealthy and the cost of this house and the servants will allow me barely enough to finish the Season."

That was not entirely true, for she had a bit of money to spare, even after she had put aside the money for Holly's dowry. Still, she could scarcely afford to pay the bills of a gentlemen about the town, even if she had wished to do so.

"Oh, no, I can manage to tog myself out properly. You need not fear you will be ashamed to be seen with me."

"I *shall* be ashamed of deceiving my friends. I have never lied before."

"Now which is worse?" His tone was reasonable. "To let people believe a lie, or to tell them one outright?"

Before she could think of a properly scornful reply, he had bowed and left the room. She could hear him in the hall, speaking to the butler. Doubtless he was preparing Hastings for his moving into the house, and allowing the servant to believe that *she* had been the one to invite him in.

Felicia ground her teeth. That—that—she could not think of words to describe him properly. It would have given her the greatest of pleasures to smash something, preferably over the villain's head. She clenched her fists and told herself she must remain calm. She had never been given to violent outbursts; it would do no good to behave so now.

When she felt she could speak calmly, she went into the hall. Hastings was making his ponderous way toward the back of the house and she called to him.

"Yes, my lady?"

"Please, Hastings, I must insist that you stop calling me 'my lady.' I am *Miss* Arsdale."

"Yes my la—Miss Arsdale. I shall endeavor to remember in the future." His tone said, "If you wish to persist in this foolishness, I must indulge you."

If he had been her old butler at home, Felicia would have given him a setdown for his manner, but Hastings seemed so much grander than the servants with whom she had grown up. Nonetheless, knowing that he had allowed that rogue to slip into the house, she was able to speak sharply, "The young gentleman who just left is my nephew. While he is in London, he will be staying with us."

"Yes, m—Miss. He so informed me." He scarcely looked a gentleman, Hastings thought, but he had spoken like one, and behaved in a properly open-handed manner.

"Then you will have a room prepared for him. I forgot to ask if he was bringing his valet." Perhaps he expected her to provide him with a servant, as well.

"He is, Miss. He informed me of that, too."

Really, the creature was taking too much upon himself. How many other "conditions" did he have in mind? "Very well." She remained calm with an effort. "You will also make arrangements for him. Now, has my niece returned?"

"She is in her room, I believe, Miss."

Felicia nodded dismissal and mounted the stairs to Holly's room. It was the first time the girl had been allowed to go to the couturière for a fitting with only her abigail to accompany her, and Felicia wondered how she had managed.

Holly was seated on the bed, surrounded by mounds of paper while Evans shook out and hung the gowns that had been sent home today. "Oh, Felicia, only see," Holly cried, reaching out to stroke the silky material. "Celestine has finished all my gowns. I can wear the new white one to Almack's."

"Of course you must wear white—Almack's. Good heavens, I forgot we were to go there tonight. I must send a message to Lady Sefton at once."

"But, Felicia, I want you to see my gowns." Holly was near to pouting at being denied her wish to show her new gowns; her sister reassured her quickly, not wishing the girl to develop a line in her flawless face.

"I shall do so in a moment, Holly. I want to speak to you, as well." She fled to her room to pen a note to Lady Sefton, explaining that the sudden arrival of her nephew ("He has my lying for him already," she muttered as she wrote) would make it impossible for them to attend Almack's this evening.

The note dispatched, she returned to Holly, to exclaim over the gowns to her sister's content. "And a number of your new gowns have come, too," Holly told her.

"That is nice. Celestine has indeed been prompt. Now, I must talk to you." A nod was enough to dismiss Evans, who showed none of the curiosity their long-time servants would have displayed.

"What is it?" Felicia appeared to be overset about something, Holly thought. Was there something about one of the gowns she disliked? The one which had the embroidery of silver acorns had seemed to her to be rather low in the neckline, but Celestine had assured her that it was quite the style.

"Something has happened, Holly—nothing to worry you," she added quickly, seeing the beginning of a frown on the younger girl's brow. She had spent so much of Holly's life making certain that nothing must make Holly unhappy, and so spoil her beauty, but it seemed more difficult to keep frowns from her sister's face since they had come to London. Or was this only a reflection of her own looks? "It is only that—that we are to have a house guest for a time."

"Oh, that will be nice," the girl said happily. "Which one of our friends is to stay?"

"It is not anyone you know. In fact, I only met him this afternoon."

"Him? You mean—a *gentleman* is going to live here with us?"

*He is certainly anything but a gentleman*, Felicia said to herself, but could scarcely say so to Holly. "I know it seems odd, Holly, but it is perfectly all right. He is—a sort of connection of ours, and wishes to stay here while he is in London. It will be a good idea, truly. Just think how nice it will be to have an escort to balls and parties. Of course, if someone else wishes to act as your escort at any time, I know Cousin Trevor will not object."

"*Cousin* Trevor?"

"Well, he is not actually a cousin. Rather a more distant relative, but it will be much easier to call him so. You will like him, I am certain."

She felt ill at ease at having to lie to Holly, and reminded herself that this was only the first of many lies she would have to tell, to Holly and to others, until that terrible Thomas creature decided he was well enough established that he no longer needed her help.

Or—until she had Holly safely married to the man she had chosen for her. Then she could tell this man to do his worst. He would never dare to malign the Honorable Mrs. James Harrison, whose father-in-law was the powerful Earl of Cranston. For herself, it did not matter what he said; she would not be in London to hear it.

Fortunately, Holly, always certain that Felicia knew best, was willing to believe this tale of welcoming a cousin they had never met and promised that she would treat him nicely. After admiring her gowns another time, Felicia made her escape from Holly's room, to see Hastings ascending the stairs.

"A message from Lady Sefton, m—Miss."

If he was going to hesitate in that fashion every time he spoke to her, people were going to be more strongly convinced than ever that she *was* Lady Felicia. She thanked him absently and took the note, surprised that Lady Sefton had taken the trouble to acknowledge her excuse for missing the evening's entertainment.

"I ought to have known it," she groaned, scanning the message. Lady Sefton had *not* accepted her excuse, but had urged her to bring her nephew with her.

"Presentable young men—and I am certain your nephew must be presentable—are always at a premium," she wrote. "Bring him, by all means."

She crumpled the message and stopped Hastings, who was halfway down the stairs. "Will you please inform Mr. Thomas that Lady Sefton has been kind enough to include him in the invitation to Almack's this evening. We shall wish to leave here promptly at half after nine, so tell the coachman to be ready at that time."

Should she warn her "cousin" that the proper attire was important for a visit to Almack's? "No," she muttered. "He will be well served if he is turned away from the door because he is wearing pantaloons rather than knee breeches."

# ∗ *Two* ∗

MUCH TO FELICIA'S satisfaction, Mr. Thomas was not present at dinner, having an engagement elsewhere; however, he had sent word that he would be prepared to accompany them to Almack's later.

Of course he will be here, she told herself. I did not doubt for an instant that he would be. He will not miss such an opportunity to be presented as he wishes. She only hoped that his manners would be better than they had been when he had been dealing with her. It would be shameful if he were to draw disapprobation from the Patronesses in any way.

For a moment, she wished she had thought to warn him about the way he must dress. If he were turned away from the door, it would reflect badly upon her—and upon Holly. Surely, he would not be so ignorant of customs as to arrive in the clothing he was wearing this afternoon. Still, he might not know that knee breeches were *de rigueur* for occasions like this evening's.

It was too late, she decided, for her to do anything now. She could scarcely send Hastings with a message reminding him to wear breeches. After all, a lady was not expected to be aware of such items of a gentleman's clothing.

Leaving Holly's preparations in Evans's capable hands

for the moment, Felicia delivered herself over to Miller, her dresser—Miller had informed her at once that she was no mere abigail—to be readied for the evening.

She would have much preferred to plead a migraine and escape the necessity of taking Mr. Thomas to Almack's, but such an action would mean that Holly must also miss the evening, for Holly could not go without her. And to miss her sister's first appearance at Almack's was something that Felicia could not allow to happen, no matter how much *she* might suffer.

Absence from an evening after vouchers and been granted would be considered an insult to all of the Patronesses, something to be overlooked only in the case of a near-mortal illness, or perhaps a death in the immediate family. It would be punished by a refusal to permit that person ever to enter those important portals. Banishment from Almack's would mean that a young lady might as well go home; she would be cut from all guest lists and the Season would be over for her.

While Miller moved competently about her tasks of preparing her for the ball, Felicia once more went over the events leading to today's confrontation with the stranger, wondering how it could have come about. It had not happened through any fault of hers, she was certain.

When she had arrived in London, there had been no thought in her mind that anyone would mistake her for her distant—very distant—kinswoman, despite their having the same name. She had stated repeatedly that she was *Miss* Felicia Arsdale, but members of the *ton* only nodded diplomatically.

As occupied as most of them were with the importance of titles, their own and others, it was difficult, but not impossible, for them to accept the fact that the heiress of the late Earl of Pendaron might be eccentric enough to wish for her own title to be unacknowledged when she arrived in

London to present her niece to their company. The lady had long been a recluse; she was not accustomed to the habits of polite society, so any sort of odd behavior might be expected of her.

Even this.

Although she continued to insist to everyone that she was *Miss* Arsdale, Felicia to owned to herself that this determination on the part of everyone to believe she was the mysterious Lady Felicia had smoothed her path. And for Holly's sake, she would permit them to believe what they wished. Nothing must be allowed to stand in the way of her plans for Holly's future.

As a child, Holly Arsdale had been prettier than most of her neighbors. At seventeen, she had bloomed into such dazzling beauty that it did not matter that she did not have a brain.

For all of Holly's life, Felicia had done her thinking for her. When she saw how beautiful the younger girl had become, Felicia knew she must not be allowed to go to waste in their small village. Or even worse, to become the wife of someone like Andrew Marsh, who was forever hanging about her.

Not that there was anything actually wrong with Andrew; he was a pleasant-spoken young man of little more than average height and much more than average handsomeness, but surely Holly could do better than to marry an apothecary's assistant, no matter how attractive he might be. Neither should she become a farmer's wife or be allowed to dwindle into an old maid. She needed someone who would care for her (and think for her), if her sister was not always able to do so.

"But we shall always be together, Felicia, shall we not?" Holly had inquired when Felicia had first mentioned taking Holly to London and finding a husband for her.

"I think we shall be," Felicia reassured her, aware that

the thought of losing the one who planned everything for her would overset the girl. "I intend that we shall, but one never knows what might happen, and we must make our plans."

"But London. It is so far away—and they say it is so large. I shall be frightened of all those people." Holly had never been shy, but it was true that the only people she knew were those who had lived near her all her life.

"There will be nothing to frighten you, Holly," the older girl assured her, stroking Holly's curls. "You know I shall see to that, as I have always done."

"But—a husband. I do not know if I should like that."

"Oh, you will not mind him at all. And you should have a husband. Look about you—most of your friends have chosen husbands."

"Why? If you do not have one—"

How could she say to the girl, but we are different? I do not *need* someone to order my life. And Holly certainly does so.

"Only think, Holly—no, do not think," she said quickly. "for it only makes you frown, and you must not do so. But can you not see how nice it would be to have someone who would care for you? Even more than I do, perhaps. And some little babes of your own."

"Oh, yes," Holly said with a wide smile, easily diverted from her worry by this new suggestion. "I like babies. They are so cuddly. And I could have them for always, could I not, if they were my own, and not have to send them home at night, as I do with Mrs. Jenkins's children. That would be nice. But, Felicia, if I should marry, what would you do? You would be left alone."

"You need not worry about what I should do, Holly. I can care quite well for myself, you know. And I shall visit with you often, of course."

She hardly planned to do anything of the kind. It would

be best if she did not attempt to involve herself in Holly's life, once she had found her the right sort of husband.

It was true enough, of course, that she could manage for herself. It was possible that their funds would be too depleted to provide for her future after Holly was married, for life in London was certain to cost a great deal. She would also have to provide Holly with a dowry, if only a small one.

If nothing remained after Holly was settled, Felicia knew she could always work as a companion to some old lady. She did not contemplate such a future with anything other than resignation, but for Holly's sake, she would do what she must.

Although she was well read, Felicia doubted that she would be considered accomplished enough to be a governess. She had taught Holly, but had been content to give her the minimum of education, which was all her sister could keep in mind. Holly would never need to learn languages or history. And there was no need to teach her deportment, for Holly was a sunny child who was always willing to obey what she was told. Also, teaching one's sister was quite a different thing from teaching strange children.

Now and then Felicia had given some thought to marriage for herself, but had always shrugged the idea away as impossible of fulfillment. Even at eighteen, when their parents died together in a carriage accident, she had ten-year-old Holly to consider, to be both mother and father to the child, so had no time for anyone else. And now, at five-and-twenty, Felicia knew she was definitely on the shelf.

She had always told herself, without the slightest jealousy, that no one would give her a second glance when Holly was about. What chance had a tall, fairly rugged form, compared to Holly's doll-like petiteness? What chance had light brown hair with only the tiniest hint of a wave, compared to shining copper curls? Or clear hazel eyes as opposed to Holly's wide blue ones? Or her determined mouth and chin compared to Holly's rosebud lips?

That was the lowering picture Felicia had of herself. Actually, she was quite pretty enough that she might have attracted any number of young men—except for one thing.

She was too intelligent.

No man would wish it known that the lady of his choice was brainier than he. Even less would he like it when her superior brain was demonstrated by the lady in question, as Felicia always managed to do, sooner or later. But why should she not do so, she always asked herself, when her superiority was so clear? So one would-be suitor after another had faded away.

The fact that she frightened these men away by showing her good sense had never worried Felicia. It was nothing more, in her mind, than good riddance of unworthy suitors. She wanted none of them for herself, having no time to spare for them. Still less did she want any of these aspiring swains for Holly.

Since it appeared to her that most gentlemen were lacking in intelligence—at least, the ones she had met—the best thing would be to find Holly a husband who was wealthy enough to employ others to manage his affairs. None of that sort had been available in Leamington.

"That is why we must go to London. And without any more delay. There must be any number of wealthy gentlemen there. And only think, Holly, you may have all the beautiful gowns and fripperies you wish—and from the finest shops in the city. All the sweetmeats you like, to nibble on—and I have heard there are shops that sell flavored ices. We can never have such things if we remain here."

"How can we go to London—just the two of us?" It was true that Felicia was able to manage everything as long as they were at home, for she had always done so. But would this not be different? Even Felicia had never been to London; how would she know what they must face?

"Certainly we can do so. I can see to everything, as I have always done here and the two of us shall have a wonderful time. There will be balls and beautiful things to see and—"

"But Maude,"—this was a neighbor's daughter who had already had one unsuccessful Season—"says that one must have an older woman to accompany one to balls and such places."

"Well, I am certainly older, so I can be your companion."

Holly's pretty brow wrinkled in a manner that caused Felicia some concern. She was trying to think again, and that was fatal. Holly *must not* develop lines on her lovely face. "No, I mean *much* older than you. Maude's aunt chaperoned her, and I am certain she must be at least fifty. And she did not approve of any of the gentlemen Maude liked."

Since the objective of the London Season had been to find Maude a husband, Felicia supposed that Maude must have chosen some entirely unsuitable gentlemen, or her aunt would not have refused to consider any of them.

"I do not think we shall have any trouble," she said. Holly had something Maude did not—the asset of great beauty.

Holly had continued to worry about the problem. "If we need to have an older lady, as Maude did, how shall we go about finding one? And what if we do not like her?"

"You are right, that might pose a problem. A strange lady would not do for us at all, and would merely be an extra expense which we can scarcely afford. I am certain we can manage quite well without her."

Above everything, a strange lady would not see that Felicia must think for her sister. She might not agree with her plans for Holly, might wish to be the one to decide who would be a suitable match for the girl. This was something she would not trust to any other. "I have it! We shall not need anyone else. I shall be the older lady."

"I know you are quite old, Felicia, but I do not think you are old enough."

Felicia hid a sigh at the thought of being considered "quite old," even by Holly. Of course, if she were seeking a husband for herself, she would be too old. But that was not the case. "I could not manage to do so as myself, of course. But if I donned a gray wig and called myself your aunt, it would be just the thing."

Many people might have found flaws in such a plan, but Holly was so accustomed to having Felicia manage everything for her that she agreed enthusiastically. The thought of wearing beautiful gowns and attending balls was quite enough to dampen any fears she might have about meeting so many people.

Clearly, Felicia could not purchase the needed gray wig in Leamington, for no one there must know of their plans. Nor could she wait to find it until she arrived in London, since she must make her first appearance as the older lady.

Visits to shops in several of the nearby villages proved to be unsuccessful, but at last, she was able to find exactly the wig she wished. The salesgirl risked losing a sale by deploring the need to cover her lovely hair and protested that it would make her appear older, but Felicia assured her that it was needed for a masquerade.

In the wig and her soberest gown, she journeyed to London to find a proper house to hire for the Season. There she faced her first problem. Not many houses were available, she learned, for most people had made their arrangements far in advance of their arrival. At last, she located one in Grosvenor Square, the family who had planned to take it having to cancel their journey due to the sudden illness of the eldest member.

The house was large for just the pair of them, but Felicia could see numbers of visitors. There was even a small ballroom, and Felicia had no trouble in visualizing Holly being partnered through the newest dances by a number of handsome gentlemen.

Although the fee was considerably more than she had anticipated, it was not beyond her purse, and Felicia decided it was worth the additional cost for the house was admirable for their purposes, being fully staffed. She could scarcely bring any servants from home, for all of them would know she was not Holly's middle-aged aunt. And she knew that they were chatterboxes who would give away the scheme at once. She and Holly were soon established in these luxurious surroundings and were busily making their preparations for launching Holly in the *ton*.

"But what about you?" Holly had asked, when her sister spoke of the new gowns she would need.

"Oh, I shall get a number for myself, as well," the older woman had assured her. "For my own would not do for my role as your aunt. I shall have to dress as an older lady. But yours are more important, so we will choose them first. Some of them, at least."

She had made discreet inquiries and had learned that Madame Celestine was among the leading dressmakers in the city. The unfortunate family which had originally hired the house had even made provision for a carriage and horses for the Season, and had hired a coachman, as well. This was another expense she had not anticipated. She saw at once, however, that this was a necessary one, for one could scarcely go about the city in hackneys, if one wished to give the appearance of affluence. Summoning the carriage, Felicia and Holly set out at once for the *couturière*'s establishment.

Celestine—*nee* Bridget Flannery—recognized the equipage and knew its occupants must be worthy of her personal attention, so waved away the assistant who had approached and greeted them, assuring them that they had done the wisest thing to come to her rather than to any of her competitors, many of whom were unable to see exactly what styles would fit each of their clients.

"I am Felicia Arsdale, and my most pressing need is for a complete wardrobe for my niece."

"Certainly, Lady Felicia—"

"Miss Arsdale," Felicia said firmly, the first of many times she would make this explanation.

Celestine gave her a shrewd glance which barely escaped being a wink. "I understand perfectly. And now, you wish a proper wardrobe for the young lady. And for yourself, as well?" The elder lady was certainly in need of stylish clothing, but might be too eccentric to care how she appeared.

"Certainly, for myself. But it is more important to have my niece's gowns first."

The prospect of completely outfitting two ladies of fashion, even if one was no longer young, had spurred Celestine to action. For days, there were long periods of fitting, of discussing the best fabrics and styles for every occasion, of choosing the proper accessories for each of the gowns.

When Felicia realized how costly gowns from Celestine would be, she wished for a moment that she had not agreed to have the woman make her wardrobe. Surely, she could have found a less expensive establishment for herself. Still, had she done so, rumor might have said that the Arsdales were pinched for funds. That must not happen.

The word of their arrival, and of the amount they were spending, was spread at once throughout the *ton*. The more Felicia had insisted that she was not the reclusive Lady

Felicia, but merely *Miss* Felicia Arsdale, the more heads nodded.

It was understood that her ladyship had always been something of an eccentric. Why she should wish to dispense with the use of her title was beyond the understanding of the title-conscious members of the *ton*, but it was whispered that she might well have absorbed French ideas while traveling abroad. And anyone could see what their ideas of equality had brought them. Still, eccentricity could be overlooked—even admired—in one so important as Pendaron's heiress.

Invitations had poured into the house at Grosvenor Square, many of them from families with eligible sons. The newest arrival in the city was not only extremely beautiful, but had noble connections. Lady Sefton had been among the first to admire Holly's beauty and offered to provide vouchers for Almack's.

And now, this *dreadful* man, whoever he might be, had appeared from nowhere and was threatening to ruin all her plans. He must not be allowed to do so. Felicia had spent too much time, and a great amount of money, as well, in planning for Holly's future and she would do whatever was necessary to see that her plans did not fail. Even if that meant she must sponsor him also.

"If you plan to be dressed on time, Miss, I must have your cooperation." Her dresser's sharp words cut into Felicia's thoughts and returned her to the present.

It was necessary, of course, for Miller to know that she wore a wig. Aside from Sukey, who fetched her morning tea or chocolate, no one else suspected the fact—until their "cousin's" arrival. She need not worry that either of the servants would talk—Sukey out of a instantly formed loyalty to a lady who treated her so kindly, Miller because she considered herself above the gossip of the servants' hall.

Miller arranged the wig, careful to see that every strand of Felicia's own hair was securely pinned so that it would not show, then helped her into one of her new gowns. Although older ladies were expected to dress more quietly than their younger relatives, Felicia knew that not all of them did so.

She had no wish to copy some of their more extravagant modes, but on the other hand, she could not bring herself to wear puce or other unattractive colors. Nor did she care for black, which was customarily reserved for widows, but was sometimes worn by elderly spinsters.

Lilac was an acceptable color for an elderly lady, but Felicia's gown was of so deep a shade that it barely escaped being purple. Simply cut, but with a deep ruching at the décolletage and around the edge of the demi-train, it emphasized her slim height and gave her an almost regal appearance.

She refused to wear a turban because she feared it might pull her wig askew. To most members of the *ton*, this insistence upon going about with her head uncovered was considered only another of the lady's eccentricities, therefore to be accepted without comment—at least, in public.

"Not that anyone is expected to notice how I appear," she told herself, going to Holly's bedchamber to meet her sister. Holly was certain to be the attraction of the evening in her white taffeta gown with its tracery of green leaves and pearl blossoms. Felicia had no doubt she would be besieged by admirers from the moment they entered the door.

"Do you think I look all right?" Holly asked, turning about to show the gown from all sides.

"You are lovely, as always," Felicia assured her, touching one of the coppery curls. "Now, come along; we must not be late."

Holly hurried after her, but stopped halfway down the stairs, gaping at the figure awaiting them. Felicia gave her a glance of annoyance, but realized that Holly could scarcely be blamed.

This was the younger girl's first sight of their "cousin." Even in her anger of the afternoon, Felicia had been forced to own that he had been more than usually handsome in the well-fitted riding clothes—if that had been what they were—he had worn at that meeting. Now that he was dressed for the evening in his long-tailed black coat, white satin breeches, ruffled shirt, and neatly tied cravat, she could see that he would certainly meet Lady Sefton's idea of a "presentable gentleman."

He advanced to the foot of the stairs, holding out a hand to each of them. "I should have brought you flowers," he said in an admiring voice, "not that either of you needs any embellishment, being perfect as you are. However, I was occupied with moving my few possessions and thought of nothing else. I apologize most deeply for allowing such matters to prevent me from doing my duty to my family. And I congratulate you. Such promptness is quite unexpected in ladies."

"It is not our habit to be late." Felicia's tone was so sharp that Holly looked at her in surprise. It did not seem to her that the young gentleman had said anything amiss. But then, Felicia would know more about such things than she.

Ignoring Felicia's remark, the gentleman bowed deeply over Holly's hand and said, "Ah, my dear cousin, I am so pleased to make your acquaintance at this time. Your cousin Trevor, at your service." He studied the younger girl for several moments, then said to Felicia, "You have done the wise thing to bring her to London to brighten this Season. She is an Incomparable, indeed."

"Th-thank you," Holly told him, blushing. "S-so are you."

"One does not say that of a gentleman." Felicia's tone was caustic.

"Well, if they do not do so, they should," her sister retorted, wringing a laugh from her "cousin" and even causing Felicia to smile.

"I thank you for the thought, cousin, whether it is customary to say it or no," Mr. Thomas said. "Now, shall we go? I can hear the horses, and, as you say, we ought not to be late." He took Felicia's wrap from Hastings's hands and draped it about her shoulders, then performed the same duty for Holly.

One could almost hear the silence, Felicia thought, as the three of them entered Almack's ballroom, one lady upon either of the gentleman's arms. "Not that anyone knows I am here," she said to herself. She did not mind that she was being overlooked; she wanted all eyes to be on Holly. However, she knew that quite as much attention was being given to their escort as to her beautiful sister, and she found that somewhat less pleasing.

Lady Sefton came to them at once, to welcome the ladies and to have Mr. Thomas presented to her. Holly was swept away to enjoy the first dance with a slightly foppish young gentleman and Felicia prepared to take her place among the dowagers, so her ladyship said, "If you do not mind, my dear, I shall take your nephew about and introduce him to some of our ladies."

"Not at all," Felicia said politely, happy to be freed for a moment from his attention.

"But, my lady, as much as I appreciate your kindness to me, I was planning to lead my aunt out for the first dance," he said.

Felicia shook her head, indicating her train. "No, I do not mean to dance tonight. Go and enjoy yourself." It was doubtless a part of his plan to act the role of the dutiful nephew, but she knew his interests lay elsewhere, and the sooner he accomplished them, the better pleased she would be.

He bowed to her and offered his arm to Lady Sefton, to be led away almost under the nose of Lady Jersey, who had come in their direction as soon as she caught sight of the new gentleman. It was rumored that Sally Jersey expected to receive a large measure of attention from every gentleman who attended Almack's, even before he made his bows to be other ladies. Her ladyship was no longer young and had never been beautiful, but she demanded to be treated as if she were, and due to the sharpness of her tongue, there were few who dared too disoblige her.

"Am I to understand that handsome creature is your nephew?" she asked, staring after Mr. Thomas, although he was already difficult to find among the young ladies—and their mamas—who crowded about, hoping to have him presented. Only his black hair was visible above the swaying of multicolored plumes.

"Yes—my sister's son, Trevor Thomas."

"Ah, a Welsh name, is it not?"

Whatever Lady Jersey heard, she would bruit about the *ton* at once, so this was Felicia's opportunity to provide the man with the credentials he wished. Perhaps they would be rid of him so much the sooner. "Yes it is—my sister's husband was Welsh. That is why we have not seen the young man for some years."

Fortunately, the noble branch of the Arsdale family had a passion for privacy, so Felicia was certain no one in London would know whether or not the late earl had more than one daughter.

"Then he and your lovely ward are brother and sister?" her ladyship persisted.

"No." She would not permit him to be Holly's brother, even for the sake of the masquerade. Best, however, not to invent *another* sister. Someone was certain to become suspicious of too many previously unheard-of relatives. "In truth, they are scarcely related. Holly is actually the daughter of one of my distant cousins, but has lived with me for many years, so I have found it much simpler to call her my niece."

"Then, as you say, they are not too closely related. That is nice, for they make such a handsome pair."

Felicia followed Lady Jersey's gaze to see that Holly was indeed dancing with Mr. Thomas. At least, they were in the same set, although she did not think he had actually partnered her.

"They do look well together," she owned reluctantly. "But, of course, nothing will come of that. We have other plans for Holly, you may be certain."

Feeling that she had gained all the information the other would give her, Lady Jersey drifted away to pass on what she had learned. Felicia soon found herself surrounded by a number of eager ladies. Most of them were mothers of marriageable daughters, who had omitted to invite Holly to their balls, not wishing her to outshine less attractive girls.

Now, they showered their invitations upon her; some pretended that their invitations must have gone astray, or inquired archly why she had not yet sent an answer, since she must have received the invitation some days earlier. None of them failed to add, "And now you must bring along your nephew, as well."

"I shall be most happy to do so," Felicia told each of them. "Provided, of course, that he does not have other plans for that evening. You know how gentlemen are. They often prefer to attend events which do not include the ladies."

She smothered a smile as she spoke, seeing the looks of disappointment on many faces when the ladies felt that the inviations had been issued in vain, and that they might have the competition of Holly without the company of her "cousin." Felicia alone knew that he would not refuse to attend any affair which would help him to attain his ends.

She was still certain that he hoped to find himself a rich wife from among the young ladies gathered at one of the *ton* parties. If that was his purpose, Felicia would do nothing to stand in his way—as long as *he* did nothing to hurt Holly's chances.

As the crowd about her thinned, her neighbor poked her with her fan and said with a chuckle, "They are in haste to spread their nets for the boy, are they not? I cannot blame them; if I were fifty—no sixty—years younger, I should be in the market for such a catch, myself."

# ✳ *Three* ✳

DESPITE HER CHAGRIN at this tribute to the young man's popularity, which equalled Holly's, Felicia smiled at the speaker, whom she had met several times at other events. Lady Brompton must be almost eighty years old, but there were times when she seemed to be more spirited than the granddaughter she was chaperoning.

Celia Burley, who had not been introduced to Felicia, appeared to be quite popular with the gentlemen, perhaps because of her grandmother's fortune, but Felicia thought she always seemed to have something on her mind, other than her latest partner. Or was it merely that she appeared more reserved compared to Holly's illusive look of interest?

The old lady almost dripped diamonds; the massive necklace about her wrinkled throat was rumored to have been the gift of some long-ago princeling—in return for certain favors not so much as whispered. In her day, she had doubtless possessed the sort of beauty to win great gifts. Even now, some vestiges of that beauty remained, despite the wrinkles.

"I have no doubt, Lady Brompton, that you would be the winner in such a contest," Felicia told her sincerely, thinking it was a pity that the granddaughter, while far from being the plainest young lady in the room, had inherited

neither the looks nor the spirit. She should have no trouble
making a match during the Season, however. For the child's
own sake, Felicia hoped that she would not set her sights
upon the abominable Mr. Thomas.

The old lady chuckled again. "Ah, I had my share of
triumphs," she owned. She fingered the necklace with a
reminiscent smile. Was the tale about its being a royal gift
the truth, Felicia wondered, or had it been invented? It
might have been given to her by her husband, or she might
have purchased it herself, and started the rumor to titillate
the *ton*. Form her brief acquaintance with her ladyship,
Felicia did not doubt any of these answers could be the
correct one.

"However," Lady Brompton was continuing, "I do not
recall that I ever had such competition as the young ladies
have from your lovely niece."

Felicia murmured a disclaimer, but inwardly agreed.
Holly *was* the loveliest young female here tonight. She had
passed from one dancing partner to another without a pause,
not even being returned to Felicia's side between sets, as
was proper. However, the Patronesses were smiling, even
the usually critical Mrs. Drummond Burrell, so it appeared
that none of them disapproved of Holly's behavior.

All of the gentlemen with whom she danced appeared to
be showering her with compliments, and doubtless were
also telling her a great deal about their various interests. Her
sister knew, however, that while Holly would blush most
becomingly when praised, she would not understand one
word in ten if they talked about their horses, sports, or, in
rare cases, politics. She would gaze up at them in wide-eyed
wonder, and each of the gentleman would be certain those
clear blue depths held understanding and complete agreement with what he was saying.

"Yes, she is quite attractive. That is, if one cares for red
hair. I suppose there may be one or two who do so;

however, I believe that dark-haired beauties are said to be the fashion this year," the lady on Felicia's other side said in a condescending tone.

Felicia recalled that Mrs. Headly's daughter was the girl she had met on another occasion—the girl who had the dark hair of which her mother spoke, but it was hair which straggled about her face, despite her constant effort to push it into place. She was also the unhappy possessor of protruding teeth and a tendency to giggle at everything said to her, besides being burdened with the name of Ophelia.

Mrs. Headly was in the habit of boasting on every occasion about her connection—many, many times removed, if she had been willing to tell the truth about the matter—with a personage "who, if he had his rights, would be sitting on the throne today." Felicia had learned earlier that the woman was a snob, and knew that it was only because she believed that Felicia was the heiress of Pendaron that she condescended to speak to her.

"Who is this important connection of whom she speaks?" Felicia asked Lady Brompton in an undertone, thinking that, since Ophelia was evidently well endowed—with money, if not with looks—she might do well enough as a wife for her "nephew."

The girl was unlikely to attract anyone who was not interested in her fortune. And a fortune hunter might not be as greatly concerned with his wife's appearance as with the size of her dowry. Yes, Trevor Thomas and Ophelia Headly would be well matched. She wondered if there was anything she could do to further the match.

"A nobody, really, despite what we are told. His ancestor—he claims—was one of the many children of Charles II."

"But—"

The old lady nodded. "On the wrong side of the blanket, of course, as all of them were. Even the Duke of Monmouth, who *claimed* his mother and father were married. Which naturally removes any of that line from pretensions to the throne. Even if the man *is* so descended, for which we have only the lady's word."

She had made no effort to moderate her tone, and Mrs. Headly rewarded her with an angry glance and stalked away to take her place farther along the line, where she could talk about her quasi-royal relative without his lineage being questioned. Felicia and Lady Brompton exchanged glances of amusement, and Felicia thought that *her* connection with a noble family was real enough, although far more distant than most people believed.

"May I have the honor of leading you out for the next dance?" a voice murmured, almost in her ear.

Felicia looked up in surprise at the speaker who was bending over her, a gentleman of about thirty years of age, quite tall, fair-haired, and thin, and not particularly handsome. James Harrison, however, had something more than appearance to offer in the marriage mart. He was the second son of the Earl of Cranston, who was rumored to be the third wealthiest man in England.

James would never have more than an "Honorable" to his name, but he would have a great deal of money and acceptance by the *ton*. Felicia had decided at once that he was the proper man for Holly.

"Thank you for the offer, sir, but I do not dance tonight." Nor any night, of course. She regretted the fact, for she had enjoyed her few opportunities to dance, but it was one of the penalties of her role as chaperon to be forced to watch, rather than taking a part in the festivities.

"Then, if you do not object to having my company for a time—" He took the chair Mrs. Headly had so recently vacated, and beamed at her. Felicia reminded herself that protruding teeth made less difference in a man's appearance than in a girl's—and his were not nearly so bad as Ophelia's.

"Would you not prefer to dance with my niece, Holly?" she asked him, indicating the girl who was passing quite near them in the set. Despite the fact that he was almost five years her senior, there was something puppyish about the gentleman which Felicia thought was quite appealing. *That is, if one does not compare him to Mr. Thomas*, she amended, then wondered how she could have compared that blackguard to a gentleman like the one at her side. There was certainly nothing appealing about her "nephew."

"No," Mr. Harrison was saying, "I should much prefer to remain here and talk with you, although I shall go away, if that is your wish. Also, if I am not being too bold on such short acquaintance, I should also like your permission to call upon you."

"Permission granted, of course. Holly will be most happy to see you."

"Ah, but it is you I wish to see, my lady." He spoke in a low tone, so that only those seated nearest to them could hear, but the softness did nothing to disguise the ardor in his voice.

Embarrassed by his attention, Felicia said, "Please—do not call me that. It is my wish to be known only as *Miss* Arsdale." As she said the words, she realized that, by her phrasing, she was guilty of allowing everyone to think she *was* her titled relative. It seemed that Mr. Thomas had been correct in his accusation that she was using everyone's confusion about the name to her advantage.

"Ah, but I will think of you as my lady. If only I could say that you were."

She stared at him, attempting to hide her feelings. This young man, the one she had chosen for Holly, appeared to be smitten with *her*!

A chuckle from Lady Brompton, who had, of course,

been an eager witness to the entire exchange, roused Felicia and reminded her that the gentleman was still expecting an answer from her.

"I—I scarcely know what to say, Mr. Harrison. You know, of course, that you are welcome to call upon us at any time. Oh, have you met my nephew, Trevor?" she added with a sense of relief she had never thought she would feel in his presence, as Mr. Thomas approached them, with Holly upon his arm.

"No, I have not yet had that pleasure," James Harrison rose to his feet, bowing to Holly and shaking hands with the newcomer.

"I fear I have not been introduced to any *gentlemen* this evening." There appeared to be a glint of amusement in Mr. Thomas's eyes as he looked down at Felicia. "Except of course, for the few who were forced to meet me because they had sisters clinging to their arms and prodding them in my direction."

"Not surprising, at all, as I told your aunt earlier," Lady Brompton said with a smile. "We could see how the nets were being spread for you. And I own I should have been doing the same as they if I were much younger. May *I* not also have the pleasure of the young man's acquaintance, my dear?"

"Oh, certainly, my lady. Lady Brompton, I should like to present my nephew, Trevor Thomas." She cast a quelling glance at Holly, who had been about to day, "I thought you said he was our cousin."

Holly knew she was being silenced, although she did not understand the reason. Doubtless, Felicia would explain later, if Holly did not forget to ask her. There was so much to remember, especially since they had come to London, that she could not always do so.

"I am honored indeed to make your acquaintance, Lady Brompton." Trevor Thomas bowed and raised to his lips the beringed hand which she offered him. "I think I may have had the pleasure earlier this evening of a dance with your lovely granddaughter."

"Not much pleasure to it, if you would tell the truth. The gel is about as graceful on the dance floor—I was about to say, as a horse. But the horses at Astley's Royal Ampitheatre are much more graceful dancers. Gels today cannot compare with what they were when I was young—except for you, my dear."

She beamed at Holly as she spoke. The girl blushed and stammered her thanks, then turned to Felicia. "I vow I must have danced with every gentleman in the rooms tonight. It has been wonderful."

"I do not think you danced with Mr. Harrison, did you, Holly?" The older girl glanced at the gentleman at her side, who ran his hand through his fair hair and fidgeted at the mention of his name.

"Oh, I am certain I must have done so, for I had so many partners. Did I not?"

"We met during the figures of a dance—several times— that is all. But I have been most happy sitting here with your aunt."

"You see, chit, not everyone prefers your company," Mr. Thomas said in a rallying tone to Holly, who only laughed.

"Enough of them did so, it seems. And all of them wished to talk about so many things that I could not begin to understand. It is puzzling."

"That is to be expected of gentlemen. Most of them do not have the wit to think that a lady might not share their interests."

Felicia threw him a grateful glance. It had been kind of him to say that, rather than laughing at Holly again. "T-Trevor is quite right about that, Holly. Although, from what we were able to observe, it seemed that none of them were too disappointed in your answers."

"I could not answer them for most of the time, but they did not appear to need answers, but simply went on talking." She slipped into the seat Mr. Harrison had vacated. "And I have danced so much that," she moved one foot cautiously, "I have worn quite through the soles of my slippers."

"In that case, perhaps it would be as well if we returned home. There will be other dances, although none to compare with your first appearance at Almack's."

"None like this, perhaps, but there will be plenty of others," Lady Brompton commented. "That is, if one can judge by the crowd of eager ladies about you earlier in the evening."

The trouble is that the greatest number of them, of course, were anxious for my "nephew's" presence, rather than Holly's, Felicia said to herself, but nodded. "Yes, I should say that we must pick and choose, for I doubt we can attend them all."

As she and Holly rose, Mr. Harrison said, "And may I be permitted to call on the morrow?"

He appeared so eager for an answer that Felicia was encouraged. He might have acted as if it was her company he preferred, but she told herself that was merely politeness on his part. When he had more opportunity to see Holly as she truly was, it would not be long before he would be making her an offer.

"You will always be welcome in Grosvenor Square, Mr. Harrison." It was Mr. Thomas who had issued the hearty invitation. As the other gentleman bowed to each of the ladies and walked away, he said in a low tone, "That was what you wished, was it not?"

"Of course," Felicia wished she might object to his attitude of being master of the house, but could see no way out of it—for the present.

They bade good night to Lady Brompton, who said, "I

should not wish to burden you with yet another invitation, as I know you must have already received more then you can possibly accept, but my granddaughter is teasing me to give a ball for her, and I suppose I must do so. I should like you to come—all of you."

"We should be most happy to do so," Felicia assured her.

"Even if it means refusing other invitations, you may be certain we shall come," her "nephew" said, bowing once more over the old lady's hand.

"And we must plan a ball for Holly, as well," Felicia said. "Not to present her, of course, since, happily, she is already becoming well know." If I am able to play my cards properly, she said to herself, it may be a ball to announce her betrothal.

"But you must not leave it too late in the Season," Lady Brompton warned. "After the Prince Regent leaves for Brighton, everyone of importance will follow him, or return home for the summer. London will be thin of company when that occurs."

"We must certainly have it before that time, so that we may have a crowd."

"And it will be difficult to find an evening which is not already crowded with balls. I am certain you have noticed that. There are so many more people than there are evenings in the Season, and no one wishes to be left out. Of course, I have no doubt that the one I give will be well attended, although the invitations have not yet been sent." The Brompton name, as well as fear of what her ladyship might say about those who were absent, would ensure a large number of acceptances.

"And we must see that ours is the same." The news of Holly's engagement would certainly be enough to crowd the small ballroom of her house. And, of course, such news would already have spread through the *ton* before the night of the ball. "However, I think we might plan to have it rather late in the Season." This would give her more time to complete *all* her plans. If she were truly fortunate, her "nephew" would have attained his wealthy wife and be gone before that occurred.

"A splendid idea, my dear. And you may be certain that Celia and I will attend."

"We shall be delighted, Lady Brompton. It would not be complete without you. And now, I think I must take Holly home before she falls asleep."

"It was quite a successful evening all around, from what I could observe," Trevor commented later, as a footman opened their door and Hastings immediately appeared to take their wraps and pass them to an underling.

"I must agree." Except for Mr. Harrison's strange talk, she thought. If I cannot turn his attention to Holly, we may be in for some problems. Then she reminded herself once more that he had only been polite to an elderly lady, and everything would soon go as she wished. He *must* choose Holly when he had the opportunity to see her another time.

If the obnoxious Mr. Thomas had not gone as he fondly hoped he would have done, by the time Holly was settled, she could then tell him to do his worst. After that she could retire to the country with no more worries. Even *he* would not dare to say anything against the daughter-in-law of the Earl of Cranston.

"I am sorry if I proved a disappointment to you," the gentleman continued.

"A disappointment? In what way?"

"By not disgracing you in any manner. Such as not dressing properly for Almack's. Or insulting one of the Patronesses. That was what you expected of me, was it not, my dear Auntie?"

"Do not be ridiculous," she said sharply, wondering if he could read her mind or had only guessed what she might think. "Such a *faux pas* would reflect badly upon us, as you know. And I have asked you not to call me 'Auntie.' " The detestable fellow only grinned at her and tipped a salute as he made his way to his own room.

"Is he not the most handsome man you ever met?" Holly asked, looking after him.

"I am certain there are many others who are equally handsome, and ones who are possessed of other attributes than mere appearance."

"Do you really think so? I do not see how anyone could be better than he in any way. I am so happy that he decided to come to London at this time, and that he is our cousin— or almost a cousin, or whatever—"

Felicia frowned, not liking her sister's tone. Holly *must* not become interested in their abominable "cousin." That would ruin all her sister's plans for a wonderful future for her. Trevor Thomas would be no good for Holly, nor for anyone else. However, since he knew that Holly was not the niece of the true Lady Felicia, she was certain there would be no advances on his part. All she must do was to keep Holly from seeing him too often, and she would put him out of her mind.

"Well, let us not worry about him tonight. Did you not have a wonderful time?"

"Oh, yes. As I said, I danced every dance."

"And did you dance with Mr. Harrison?"

Holly attempted to cast her mind back over the numerous partners with whom she had danced. "I—I do not think I did so. But there were so many—"

Holly was so forgetful that she had no recollection of the gentleman who had been standing beside Felicia until the older woman said, "You must remember him, dear. He was the gentleman standing near us as we left—the one who asked if he might call upon us tomorrow."

"N-no, I do not believe I stood up with him. I think he

said I had not, did he not? Although I might have met him in one of the sets or other. Why?"

"Oh, no reason at all," Felicia said hastily, thinking it would be best for her to talk more to Holly about him before the gentleman called. It would be a waste of time to do so now, while the girl was so nearly asleep. It was difficult enough to keep her mind on a subject when she was at her best. "It is only that he seems a very nice young gentleman, and I wish you will be attentive to him when he calls."

"Of course—if you wish it." The younger girl made no attempt to smother a wide yawn. "I am so happy that we came to London, after all, for I am having such a wonderful time. But it does not seem that you will be able to enjoy it very much, if you are forced to sit on the sidelines every time we attend a ball."

"Never mind about me. I am well pleased when you are happy." She smothered the tinge of disappointment that she could never take a part in such affairs. But, of course, she was long past such things, even if she was not nearly the age she pretended. "Now, dear, you must rest. And so must I."

Both young ladies were accustomed to rising early at home, for there was always so much to be done. Felicia was determined, however, that she would allow Holly to sleep as long as she wished while they were in the city. There must be no chance for her to develop dark circles beneath her eyes; nor must she yawn when in company, a habit she had not yet outgrown.

For herself, sleep did not matter so greatly, but Felicia felt she was quite a slugabed when Sukey arrived with her morning chocolate and confided the information that it was after ten o'clock.

"Oh, dear, I do not believe I have ever slept so late as this. There is much to be done, although I thought when we came here, it would be a different matter. I hope my si—my niece is still abed."

"Oh, yes, and Evans gave me orders that I was not to go to her until she rang."

"That is good. She danced every dance last evening, so must have been quite fatigued." Now why was she confiding in a servant—even in Sukey? That sort of thing might do very well at home, but she must remember that life was different in London. These people did not consider themselves part of the family and did not expect to be treated as such. "And Evans is correct. The girl needs her sleep."

When she descended to the breakfast room, Felicia was unpleasantly surprised to find Mr. Thomas was still lounging at the table with the newspaper spread before him and a coffee cup in his hand, much as if he were truly a member of the family. She had hoped that he would have left the house by this hour.

"The best of mornings to you, dear Auntie," he said, rising as she entered the room. "You must indeed be proud of the impression caused by our beautiful ninny-hammer last night."

*Our*, indeed! And how dared he call Holly by such a name? "It appeared to me that you did not fare too badly yourself, when it came to attracting the attention you must have wished," she retorted in her sharpest tone.

"Ah, you noticed? I am flattered, for I did not think you were interested in my progress."

"I am not interested in whatever you do. But how could I help noticing when I was besieged with invitations, all carrying the message, 'You must bring your handsome nephew, as well'?"

"Poor Auntie." If she did not know how deceitful he could be, she might have thought him truly sympathetic. "Did no one spare a thought for you? But I forgot—there was one very attentive gentleman. The one who begged permission to call today."

"He is calling upon Holly."

Something in her tone made him look at her sharply. "Oh, is he the one you have chosen for her? I fear you may be out there. Neither of them appeared to favor the idea. Although you may persuade her to it."

"Much you know about such things, sir," she was goaded into saying.

He ignored the first part of her remark, to say, "Sir? Has it not occurred to you that it would be best for you to accustom yourself to calling me Trevor? People will think it odd if you continue to address your devoted nephew as 'sir.' "

Felicia gave him an angry look, evoking a wide smile from him. "Say it, why do you not? It is not difficult, truly it is not. Only two small syllables. I am certain you can do so if you try."

"Very well, I shall call you Trevor—when others are about. As I was able to do last evening, you may recall. When we are alone—"

"You would prefer to call me hedgebird, or something of the like."

"I should prefer not to be forced to speak to you at all."

He shook his head, but rose, placing his newspaper upon the table. "Very well, since I fear I might take away your appetite, I shall relieve you of my presence, for the moment, only, dear Aun—"

"I have told you not to call me that!"

"Is it the 'Auntie' to which you object? I suppose it is. In future, unless others are about, I shall simply call you 'dear.' "

He was out of the room before she could think of a scathing reply. It was only the arrival of Hastings at that moment which prevented her from throwing something after the scoundrel. She had never been prone to such urges, until now. "How am I to endure his insolence?" she muttered. "If only he can find the rich wife he wishes—if that is his goal—before I end in bedlam."

By the time Holly came down to breakfast, smiling as she recalled the triumphs of last evening, Felicia had regained some measure of her composure. As Holly spread a liberal thickness of butter on a muffin, she looked about the table and asked, "Has Cousin Trevor not yet come down?"

"Some time ago." What was she to do if Holly formed a *tendre* for their abominable "cousin"? Could she hope to make her forget him if he remained underfoot? "He has gone out."

"Out? Will he return?"

Felicia sighed. "Oh, yes, he will certainly return." There was a way, perhaps, to curb the other's interest in the man. "You ought to know, Holly, that he is in London in search of an heiress."

"Oh." She absentmindedly buttered a second muffin, leaving the first one half-eaten. "We are not heiresses, are we?"

"Certainly not." Felicia took up the piece of muffin her sister had discarded and nibbled at it, being forced to wash it down with a swallow of tea. She had not realized her throat had become so dry—another mark to chalk against the blackguard's account. "We have the money to pay for your Season and a bit more. But M—Trevor—is searching for a young lady with a considerable fortune. He would not be satisfied with anything less."

"I see." For an instant, it seemed that Holly would frown, but her customary sunny nature soon triumphed. "I suppose a gentleman must need a great deal of money. If that is what he wishes, I hope that he will find a wealthy lady."

"And soon." Felicia echoed the wish with fervor. "Now

that you have finished your breakfast, Holly, you must practice on the pianoforte. It may be some time before we have one at home, and you must make the most of your time here."

Despite what she said, she did not expect that it would be necessary to take Holly home; surely, the proper husband would be found for her before the end of the season. If it was not James Harrison, it would be some other of the same ilk.

Holly rose with resignation and made her way to the music room. She did *not* like to practice on the pianoforte—it was so difficult for her to remember what notes she was to play next—but most young ladies played either the pianoforte or the harp, and Holly was certain the harp would be even more difficult to learn. All those strings appeared so formidable. At least, she did not have to see the strings of the pianoforte, so she could pretend they were not there.

Felicia always knew when she had struck a wrong note. Sometimes Holly thought it a pity that it was not Felicia who was making a comeout in her place, because Felicia always knew what must be done. But then, Felicia was quite old—older than any of the debutantes of the season— and if Felicia were entering society, *she* would not have so many pretty gowns to wear or be asked to dance by so many nice gentlemen. Some of them were almost as nice as Cousin Trevor. But not quite.

Perhaps it was worth the trouble of learning to play the pianoforte in order to have so nice a Season. She struck three wrong notes in succession, surprised herself by recognizing that she had made an error, and began once more.

Felicia had brought some embroidery into the room and sat, listening to Holly's attempts. Would she ever be able to play properly? Of course, most of the young girls she had heard were almost as bad, it seemed, but she would like for Holly to do better than the others.

"B flat," she said as another mistake rang in her ears. "That is the black key—no, the other one. Can you not hear the difference?"

"I doubt if I shall ever learn," Holly said, making the correction.

"Of course you can." The assurance came in hearty tones from Trevor Thomas, who had returned to the house in time to hear the last remark.

He did not believe for an instant that she could do so, for it seemed she knew nothing of music. It was cruel to force the girl to attempt something that was so far beyond her powers. From what he had been able to observe, the producing of even passable music was far beyond the powers of most young ladies, but that did not prevent proud mamas from forcing them to play, and their callers to listen on every occasion.

"Oh, do you think so?" Holly gave him a radiant smile. She had completely forgot what Felicia had said about his seeking a wealthy wife. Not that she felt any deep interest in the gentleman nor in any other. The only important thing was that *this* handsome man was encouraging her, making her feel that she was not so stupid, after all.

"Certainly. It only takes a bit of time. Now, can you play a waltz?"

"Oh—oh, yes." One of the four pieces Holly could make her way through with a minimum of false notes was in waltz time. She began to play it at once.

"Come, Auntie." Trevor hid a grimace at the discords as he turned to Felicia. "You did not dance at all last evening. Let us enjoy a dance now." Before Felicia could retort that she did not wish to dance, especially with him, he had caught her hand and pulled her to her feet, spilling her embroidery silks in all directions as he whirled her about the room.

"Stop this at once!" Felicia cried, attempting to free herself from the arm which held her so tightly. "I do not wish—"

"Now, that is not the way to behave when a man asks you to dance, my dear Au—Oh, I forgot. Still, need I remind you that you should say, 'Yes, thank you.'? You will be giving Holly the wrong idea of how to act." He was carrying her about so swiftly that Felicia was completely out of breath.

Then she stopped struggling, realizing that he was an excellent dancer and that it was a pleasure to be partnered by him. It had been so long since she had danced with anyone that she had fallen into the habit of convincing herself that she would no longer enjoy it. How could she have fooled herself so completely? And this waltz, which she had never danced before, was so exhilarating.

Holly, in her attempts to watch their performance, was striking more wrong notes than usual, when Hastings appeared in the doorway to announce, "Mrs. Headly and Miss Headly."

Scarcely waiting for the man to pronounce her name, Mrs. Headly had rushed into the room, Ophelia upon her heels. The pair stopped, gaping at the whirling couple.

Her face crimson at being found in such a state, Felicia managed to free herself from the constricting arm. "Good day, Mrs. Headly," she said, gasping for breath, then, "Oh, Holly, please stop. We have guests."

The older lady, however, was in far too great a flutter to notice anything amiss. "Oh, Lady Felicia, I must apologize for breaking in on you in this way—"

"Not at all. And please, it is *Miss* Arsdale."

Mrs. Headly tittered. "Of course. I forgot that you

wished not to use your title. But in my excitement. . . .
Have you heard about poor Lady Brompton?"

"What happened? Is she ill?"

"Not really, but she must be prostrated. I know I should
be in the circumstances."

"In what circumstances?" Could the woman never come
to the point?

"You have not heard, then? Last night, someone—some
thief entered her house. And stole her magnificent diamond
necklace—*from the dressing table in her bedchamber.*"

# * Four *

"HOW TERRIFYING! I hope that Lady Brompton was not injured."

"No, she says that she slept through the entire affair—if that is what you would call it. I do not see how she could have done so." Mrs. Headly's tone accused her ladyship of having a lack of sensibilty. "I know *I* should have felt it at once if such a malignant presence entered my room."

"And I. I should have *died* of fright," Ophelia said, and giggled.

Her mother caught her arm, shaking her roughly. "Stop that, you goose. What will La—Miss Arsdale think of you, behaving in such a way? Although I must own that the thought of a strange man entering my bedchamber is enough to put me in a fright."

"I should not think that either of them would ever have cause to worry about *that*," Trevor murmured in Felicia's ear, causing her to choke violently to prevent herself from bursting into laughter. How dared he be so insensitive about others' feelings—even those of foolish people like Mrs. Headly and her daughter—and so correct in his comments about them?

For the moment, she forgot that she had hoped that Trevor would marry Ophelia, thus removing both of them from the London scene. Then she remembered, and was forced to choke down another laugh at the thought of those two, so mismatched, except that he wished money and Ophelia wished for a husband.

When she had recovered her breath, aided by Trevor's solicitous, but none too gentle, pats on her back, she said, "Oh, we must send word to Lady Brompton at once to see if there is anything we can do for her."

"Yes, that is what we should do. I should be more than happy to accompany you, La—Miss Arsdale. We must all join in showing her ladyship how greatly we sympathize with her loss."

Thinking that, in like circumstances, the last person she would wish to see would be this garrulous woman, Felicia said, "Well, I had not actually thought of visiting her at this time."

"But you said—"

"What I meant to say was that it would be the best thing if we should merely plan to leave a message at her house which would convey our sympathy for her loss and our offer of assistance, but without any expectation of seeing her. Lady Brompton doubtless has already received a great number of callers this morning, and I feel certain she will not welcome any others."

Bitterly disappointed at the thought that she would not be permitted to pay a call upon the victimized lady in such illustrious company, Mrs. Headly gabbled on for some moments about the theft, repeating only what she had said earlier, then left to see if she might be the first to carry the news of the daring theft elsewhere.

"Can you imagine what it must be like to have to listen to that idiot child giggling all the time?" Trevor asked. "Which would be worse, her giggling or her mother's never-ending chatter?"

So much for her idea of paring Trevor with the girl,

Felicia told herself, as she and Holly hurried to prepare for their call.

She was correct in thinking that Lady Brompton's butler would be turning away hordes of curious callers with the word that her ladyship was much too overset by what had happened to see any visitors today. However, when Felicia attempted to leave her message, she was told that Lady Brompton had given orders to admit her and her party, should they happen to call.

She expected that the old lady would be prostrate upon her bed after having undergone so harrowing an experience. To her great surprise, however, Lady Brompton awaited them in the saloon, looking much the same as she had done last evening. She was gowned as if she planned to attend some gala affair rather than as if she were expecting callers, and her many rings glistened upon either hand. Only the famed diamond necklace was missing.

"My dear Felicia—," she exclaimed, extending a hand as the visitors entered, "if I may be permitted to call you so upon such short acquaintance—it was so kind of you pay me a call."

By the use of her caller's first name, she was able to gloss over the necessity of deciding whether or not she ought to call her, "Lady Felicia," since she had learned last evening that the lady did not approve of the usage of a title. And in view of her own great age, one could not consider that this informality comprised an impertinence.

"I do not doubt half of London has already called upon you today," Felicia said with a smile. "It was with some difficulty that I dissuaded Mrs. Headly from accompanying me."

"I am happy you were able to do so, although it must have taken an enormous effort on your part to shake her loose. In addition to being a toadeater, the woman is a bore and a gossip monger."

"What a dreadful combination of characteristics," Felicia said, laughing.

"Yes, is it not? But I am being quite accurate, I assure you. I am certain she has run over half of London by this time, attempting to convey the impression that she knows the full details of the theft."

"It would not surprise me if you were correct in that, for she told us every detail she knew—several times. And I am certain we should never have been able to escape having her accompany us, even by telling her rudely that she was not welcome, if she had suspected that we should be allowed to see you. I did not expect that myself, knowing your situation, but had merely planned to leave a message asking if I might be of any assistance."

"No, there is nothing anyone can do, I fear. Except locate my missing diamonds. And that is beyond all our powers."

"I must own that, like everyone else, I was prompted to call by vulgar curiosity about the events of last evening."

"If you said anything else, I should suspect you of lying," Lady Brompton said with a laugh. "Although most of my friends would not own to such a failing, but would have given some flibbertigibbet excuse for the call. But I am happy to see you here, my dear. And your two young ones, as well." She again extended her hand, which Holly touched with an inarticulate murmur and a blush. Trevor, in his turn, bowed over the hand and expressed his sympathy at her loss.

A young lady came hurriedly into the room, stopping when she saw the callers. Despite her youth, she was much more graceful than one would have supposed after hearing Lady Brompton's unkind comments about her dancing. Felicia suspected that had been merely her ladyship's way of trying to hide her pride in the girl. "Oh, I had not meant to intrude, Grandmama," she said. "I thought you were not at home to anyone today."

"I thought I might make some exceptions in the case of good friends, even if they are new ones. And you know you can never intrude, my dear, whatever I may be doing. I do not believe you have met my granddaughter before, have you, Felicia?"

"No, I have seen the young lady, but did not have the pleasure of meeting her last evening, nor upon other occasions as well, for it seemed that she was taken for every dance each time."

"*Miss* Felicia Arsdale, please allow me to present my granddaughter, Celia Burley." The old lady's eyes twinkled at the two of them as she made the presentation. Like the rest of the *ton*, she thought Felicia's refusal to use a title nothing more than an affectation, but, since she had always done exactly as she pleased, she considered Felicia had a right to do the same.

Celia was a rather pretty young lady with glossy black curls and merry black eyes. Everything, Felicia said to herself, that Mrs. Headly wished her daughter to be. Like Holly, she was in her first Season, and appeared to be enjoying every moment of it, despite her reserved demeanor in public. She curtsied prettily to Felicia, acknowledged the introduction to Holly, then said to Trevor, "Oh, yes, sir, I believe we danced last evening."

"I had that pleasure," he said with a smile, "but only for one dance. You were too popular for me to be granted another, even if such a thing had not been beyond the bounds of propriety."

"Fiddlesticks," her grandmother interrupted. "Handsome as you are, young man, I am certain you know that any girl with an ounce of wit would have said, 'propriety be hanged,' and made some excuse to dance with you again, had you asked her. And doubtless made some excuse to slip out into the garden with you, had there been one—which they know better than to have at Almack's, for no one would remain on that terrible dance floor."

"Well, I should have begged another dance, at least, if given the opportunity." The blue eyes gleamed, sharing the old lady's amusement. "Although I should have asked *you* to be my partner, as well."

"And you think I should not have accepted? Let me tell you, young man, even at my age, I can still step a pretty measure. But I should have insisted upon waiting for that naughty waltz. There was nothing like it when I was young, I am sorry to way. I suppose you have enjoyed it, however, Felicia."

"Well—" Felicia felt her color rising, thinking of the moments when she was whirled about in Trevor's arms, and knowing the sort of look he was doubtless casting her way. "I must own to have done so—once. But not in public—it was not done when I was Celia's age."

"More pleasant if done in private, I have no doubt," the old lady commented. Trevor chuckled, and Felicia—not for the first time—felt a strong urge to strike him. Preferably with something heavy.

"Oh, a waltz can be pleasant at any time, that is, if one has the proper partner who does not step on one's feet," Celia said. "Do you not agree?" she asked Holly.

"Oh, yes. I was so happy when Lady Sefton gave me permission to do the waltz, for it would have been terrible if I had been the only one who was not dancing. Although some of the gentlemen wish to talk about such bewildering things."

"I do not doubt that," Lady Brompton commented drily.

It was clear to her that it would take very little to bewilder this beautiful young girl. Her granddaughter might not equal the copper-haired Beauty in appearance, but her mind was doubtless much sharper. Any grandchild of mine, she told herself, must have at least a part of my wit. It was as well that Holly had her clever aunt to see that she found the right match.

"Now," she ordered Trevor, "take the children off to the far side of the room and amuse them for a time. I should like a pleasant coze with Felicia."

The gentleman bowed, caught each of the young ladies by the hand and led them away. Lady Brompton watched them go, her eyes twinkling.

"I wonder which of your charges you will succeed in firing off first."

"Oh, well, you must understand that Trevor is not exactly in my charge."

"But you are presenting him to the *ton*?"

"Certainly. It is his wish and one can do no less for a relative. But a gentleman of his age can well shift for himself, and I do not doubt he would prefer to do so. However, he has thought it would not be proper for Holly and myself to live in London without some—some man of the family—to look after us, so he came to us as soon as he arrived in the city. I should not doubt that he will be leaving us before too long." At least, I can hope that he will do so, she said to herself.

"And doubtless will break a score of hearts when he makes his choice."

Felicia murmured something which might have been taken for assent. The scoundrel *was* devastatingly handsome, she owned to herself, hoping that neither of the girls talking with him now would be among his victims. He would not try to capture Holly's interest, knowing that she had no fortune. But that did not mean he could not interest her without making an attempt to do so.

Should she warn Lady Brompton that she ought to protect her granddaughter from his attentions? And could she do any such thing without betraying the fact that Trevor was *not* her nephew, but was a complete stranger who had forced her to introduce him to the *ton* by threatening to ruin her plans for Holly?

Still, she was certain that the old lady was clever enough not to be taken in by mere handsomeness and would guard her granddaughter well. Best to leave well alone, before he was driven to retaliating.

"But never mind about him," she said. "As I said, Trevor can manage quite well for himself. And I am certain he will do so. As I said, I am fairly eaten with curiosity about the thief who stole your lovely necklace. Although I doubt you could tell me much more than the gossips already know."

"Not by so much as a word. In truth, it would not surprise me if they were already telling much more about it than truly happened. Why he did not take all my jewels, I cannot understand, for they were all together."

"Perhaps he hesitated to take your rings because they would be too easily recognized."

"Oh, you mean that he could take the stones out of the necklace so that no one would know them? Even if they were handled separately, they would be worth a great deal. Of course, he could have done that with the rings, but there were not nearly so many stones. I could wish, however, that he *had* taken the other things instead. That necklace has always had an especial meaning for me, and I dislike the thought that it might be broken up."

"Or perhaps he might have been frightened off," Felicia said, more to ease her ladyship's mind than because she thought this the true reason. "Did you rouse—or perhaps you might have stirred enough to make him think you had awakened?"

"I wish I had done so."

"Oh, no, Lady Brompton. You might have been in great danger if he knew you had seen him."

"Nothing of the kind! Had I known he was there, I should have thrown my candlestick at him. Should have hit him too. And heavy as it is, he would not have escaped, I tell you."

The vigor in the old lady's tone made Felicia laugh. "I do not doubt you would have routed him easily enough. But a thief interrupted at his work may be dangerous."

"Most certainly he would be," Trevor said, having returned to them in time to hear the last remarks. "It was much better for you, dear lady, that you were able to sleep through his visit. Even if it does mean the loss of your beautiful necklace. I had an opportunity to admire it last evening."

"Why are you not amusing the children as Lady Brompton told you?" Felicia wanted to know. She had been enjoying the conversation until he joined them.

"Oh, they ordered me away. Wanted to exchange female talk. Just as I suppose the two of you are doing. Such is the fate of a poor man in this world—never to be wanted anywhere." He spoke mournfully, as if hoping for pity, but Lady Brompton only laughed.

"Nonsense, you are merely fishing for flattery. And I should not think you would need to do that. I have told your aunt that I expect you to break half the hearts in London before the Season ends."

"I should count myself a fortunate fellow indeed if yours could be counted among them."

The old lady aimed a playful slap at the hand lying upon the arm of her chair. "Hedgebird! Do you think me another Lady Jersey, that I must be made the object of your flirtation?"

"Alas, no, my lady, I think you far too clever for that. But to repeat my dear aunt's observation of several moments ago, I think you should realize how fortunate you were not to have wakened and aroused the anger of the thief."

"Oh, I do not wish to speak of it anymore." There was

more than a trace of petulance in the old lady's tone. If the necklace were truly the gift of some long-ago admirer, its loss must have meant much more to her than the value of the stones.

"No, and we should not have insisted that you do so," Felicia said contritely. "We ought not to have intruded at such a time."

"No, my dear, I wished to speak with you for a moment or so. It has been so much more comfortable than so many of my friends would have been. But I own that I am somewhat weary."

"And we have been overstaying our welcome. It was kind of you to invite us in, and we shall visit again at some other time. Come, Holly, make your adieux to Lady Brompton."

As Felicia rose, the older woman caught her hand. "No, it is only that I do not wish to talk more about the theft, for I find it too depressing. I do not mean to drive you away."

"You are doing nothing of the kind." Felicia bent and brushed a light kiss on one wrinkled cheek. "Rather you should be the one to forgive us. We are still new to the London scene and sometimes forget the limits placed upon calls."

"Nonsense! What do I care for such rules? They were made by stupid people for others who have less sense, and are best ignored. I should like you to remain longer, but in truth, this dreadful experience has wearied me. Before you go, however, I wish you will promise me to bring your young folk to my Celia's ball."

"You know we shall be delighted to come." If only Lady Brompton knew how it rankled to have Trevor called one of her "young folk." She had not minded being thought old enough to pose as Holly's aunt; it was easier to do so than to admit a stranger to their plans, but to be considered the elder of a man who must actually be five or more years older than herself. . . . "And you have already promised that both of you will come to ours."

"Have you settled upon a date yet?"

"No, but I must do so quite soon, so that I can have my invitations out before it is too late for any sort of acceptance from our friends. Acquaintances, I should rather call the most of them."

After bidding Lady Brompton the sort of flowery farewell she must have been accustomed to in her youth and begging Celia to save him at least a dance or two at her ball, Trevor escorted the Arsdale ladies to their carriage. Taking his place facing them, he said, "One must admire the cleverness of a man who could manage to make his way into the house and garner himself such a prize without disturbing anyone."

"You mean to say that you think him clever?" Felicia demanded. "A criminal? One who might well have murdered the poor lady in her bed?"

"Oh, I doubt there was any danger of that, despite what I said to her ladyship earlier. That was merely to make her feel that she had done the best thing by remaining asleep. Thieves do not often commit murder, as far as I have been able to discover. And if the owners of such valuable pieces as that necklace do not take proper care of them, they are asking to have them stolen."

"If you are going to continue praising such a person, I trust you will have the good taste to keep your opinions to yourself."

Trevor bowed as low as his seated position would permit. "Your know your word is my law, dear Auntie. As always."

How I wish that were the truth, Felicia told herself. If it were, you would be leagues away from London. And knew, by the taunting smile he gave her, that he had divined her thoughts once more.

When they arrived home, Hastings met them with the information that Mr. James Harrison had called, adding, "He appeared to be under the impression that your—that you were expecting him to call."

"Oh, dear, that is right. He did ask if he might call upon us today, and we had extended our invitation for him to do so. When I learned of Lady Brompton's theft, everything else went completely out of my mind. Holly, you must write him to explain our absence when arrived."

"I?" Holly's eyes opened to their fullest. "What ought I to say, Felicia?"

"No, I had best do it myself." Even if her sister wrote out the words for her, Holly could not be depended upon to copy the message without making mistakes. And the earl's son must not find anything about her beautiful sister to criticize. Once they were safely married, he must certainly be willing to overlook any such small faults in one so beautiful.

"Why do you want Holly to write him?" Trevor wanted to know. "He is not interested in hearing from her."

"Do not be so foolish." And what affair was it of his, anyhow? "That is the only reason he has called on us today."

"You know better than to expect anyone to believe that, my dear Auntie. Oh, I forgot. You do not wish to be called 'Auntie,' only 'my dear.'"

"Will you stop talking such fustian?"

"It is not fustian to say that the Miss Arsdale who has won the interest of the noble gentleman is not your niece, my girl, but yourself."

As much as she would have liked to dismiss Trevor's comments from her mind, as well as dismissing the man from her life, Felicia feared he was correct. James Harrison *had* asked if he might call upon *her*. "But, of course," she said to herself, "when he said that, he was only being polite to the chaperon of the young lady he truly wishes to visit. It would be the gentlemanly thing to ask to speak to me rather than to Holly." She wished she truly believed that was his reason.

If, for some reason she was unable to fathom, he did regard her more favorably than the younger girl at the moment, he would certainly change his interest to Holly when he had more opportunity to see how lovely she was. Even without the gray wig and her attempts to appear middle-aged, Felicia knew she could never have competed with Holly, any more than she had done at home.

Her letter, apologizing for not having been at home at the time of his call, and explaining that they had merely gone to offer sympathy to Lady Brompton upon her loss and had not intended to be so long from home, should have taken only minutes to write. She was hampered, however, because they were besieged by callers, many of whom she was unable to recognize, as soon as it was learned that they had returned home.

Word had gone rapidly about the *ton* that Lady Felicia— or *Miss* Felicia, if they bowed to her eccentric wish to be so called—was the only one who had been admitted to Lady Brompton's presence. It seemed probable, therefore, that she would have a great deal more to tell about the theft than had been made public, and all London was agog for the details.

Mrs. Headly and her daughter were among the first to arrive, the girl punctuating every remark of her own or others with giggles, as usual, and the elder lady inclined to be indignant at having been excluded from the visit to the victim.

"You knew I should have been most happy to accompany you to Lady Brompton's today," she insisted, "because I told you as much. But *you* told *me* that you would only leave a message for her and would make no attempt to enter the house. And, after all, I have known Lady Brompton much longer than you have done. I would not say precisely that we were bosom bows, but our acquaintance has been a matter of some years. If anyone was to see her, *I* should have been the one to do so."

"But I assure you, my dear Mrs. Headly," Felicia said, thinking, gossipy old harridan; no wonder Lady Brompton did not wish to see her, "I had not thought that her ladyship would condescend to ask me in. And, in truth, she was unable to tell me anything that you had not already told me."

Mrs. Headly only sniffed at the other's explanation, certain that her omission from the list of favored visitors had merely been a case of Lady Brompton's being willing to talk only to another lady of title. She quite ignored the fact that Ladies Jersey, Sefton, and Melbourne had been among those who had not been favored with equal invitations to enter the house.

Felicia considered the lady's pique not worth a moment's thought, for she was far too occupied in giving the same answer to many other curious callers, most of them more polite in their questioning than Mrs. Headly, but each of them certain that she could, if she would, tell them more about the incident.

"Is it true that her ladyship did wake and see the villain?" several asked. "Was she able to describe him?" And others wanted to know if Lady Brompton had truly thrown her candlestick at the man, as they had heard, and thus chased him away before he could take anything more than the famous necklace.

"No," Felicia said more times than she could count, "Lady Brompton says that she slept through the entire theft, which, I am certain, was the best thing she could have done."

# * Five *

"BUT IF SHE had known he was in the room," one lady exclaimed, "she might have rung for a servant and caught the man."

"No," another said. "Such a thing would have been much too dangerous. Who knows what the thief might have done if he realized he was being observed? If a man is so depraved as to stoop to a life of burglary, it can only be a few more steps to murder."

"I doubt that he would have done anything of the kind," Trevor said from the corner where he was surrounded by another curious crowd, a number of them gentlemen, and all of them hoping that he might supply them with more exciting information than his aunt was telling their ladies. "As I told my aunt earlier, one seldom hears of thieves who commit murder."

"But you cannot be certain that he would be content with merely taking her jewels." The lady who had spoken of possible danger said triumphantly, as if scoring a point off a gentleman was a matter of prime importance to her. "If he thought there was even a chance that she might be able to describe him—"

"No, I doubt that anyone could could give you a true answer to what he might have done in those circumstances, except the thief himself."

"So it could have happened."

"Certainly, it could have done," he owned, "although I doubt it. However, I fear what might have been Lady Brompton's reaction had she truly seen such a man making off with her jewels. She thinks she would have attempted to apprehend him, but the shock of finding a prowler in her room might well have been more than she could bear. We all know she is a brave lady, but after all, she is no longer young and something of that kind could have had a bad effect upon her health."

A number of the callers were quick to agree with him; others were equally certain that Lady Brompton would have kept her head, regardless of the situation, and would have done exactly as she said.

When the last reluctant caller had been ushered out by Hastings, still flinging questions over the butler's shoulder, Felicia sank into a chair with a sigh. "Why is it," she asked, "that people will not believe what they are told? All of them were certain before they arrived that we knew some secret about Lady Brompton's missing necklace. One would think that we had been hiding in her cupboard and had actually seen the thief."

"This is not the first time you have had problems with people believing what they wished, is it?" Trevor asked. The words seemed to be idly spoken, but she sensed a deeper meaning beneath them.

Was he referring to her scheme for launching Holly in the *ton*, or to his own masquerade as her nephew? Not that anyone had appeared to doubt *that* part of their deception. Had he been less handsome, she wondered if he would have been accepted quite so eagerly, even if he had her sponsorship.

As for people not believing what she had told them about herself and Holly, she secretly owned that she had been happy that they had leaped to the wrong conclusion. It had helped her enormously, until Trevor had come upon the scene.

Several barbed retorts arose to Felicia's mind, but she told herself that it would be unladylike for her to stoop to exchanging remarks with him. Also, she was prevented from making them by the presence of servants in the room. Servants, she knew from experience, were all too prone to exchange gossip with their friends about the doings of their respective employers, and she wished to give them no such tidbits about the members of her "family" to pass along to their friends.

Wearily, she returned to the missive to be sent to James Harrison, but was interrupted again, only a few moments later. Lady Brompton's granddaughter had arrived, accompanied by her elderly maid.

"I know it is somewhat past the time for visits," Celia said in her customary breathless manner, as if she feared to be thought too coming in her ways. "But Grandmama thought you would not mind if I came to spend some time with Holly. I think perhaps she—I mean Grandmama, of course, not Holly—is more overset by the theft of her necklace than she wishes anyone to know, and would like to be alone for a time."

"My dear child," Felicia told her warmly. "You are welcome to come here at any hour, and need no excuse to call upon us. I only wish that we were able to do something to save your grandmama from the crowds of curious people who appear to think she can tell them exactly who took the necklace. We have been besieged by callers who think she has told us much more about the theft than has already reached the public."

"I am sorry to hear that they have been worrying you, and I know Grandmama will be, as well."

"There is nothing that can be done about the curiosity of our friends and acquaintances," Trevor told her and received a grateful glance from Felicia and a warmer one from Celia.

"Grandmama has given orders now that all callers are to be told she has taken to her bed, overcome by the vapors. Not that it is true, of course, because I am certain that Grandmama has never had the vapors in her life, and would not have them even if she *had* seen the thief. But, at least, no one dares insist upon an entrance."

"That was a very wise thing for her to do. Curious people can be so worrisome, especially when she already has much to worry her. I have felt that we, too, were imposing upon her good nature when we called."

"Oh, no, she wished to see you and told me that she had enjoyed your visit. But there have been such crowds about the house all day. And not only people we know; that would be bad enough, although one can understand their curiosity. But there must be half of London there this afternoon."

"That is much too bad. How could total strangers come to know about such things?"

"I suppose everyone's servants have been gossiping, so that salespeople and others of their kind have learned everything there is to know. And have added to the tale as they passed it along."

"Yes, that could be one way for the stories to be spread." Had she not thought the same thing about their own servants only moments ago?

"One cannot help overhearing what they say, of course, and there are some who have said Grandmama was to blame for what occurred because she did not take better care of her necklace."

Felicia shot an angry glance at Trevor, but he shook his head, as if to convey that he had not voiced such a thought to anyone but her. "There are certain to be those who say that," he told Celia. "Doubtless they are people who have never had any valuables to lose."

"I suppose you are right about that, but it was only a necklace, after all. And Grandmama has so many other jewels. They will all be mine someday, I believe. And I would not have wished to wear that necklace. It is so heavy. I think it quite ugly, too, although Grandmama does not."

"So whoever took it has in truth done you a favor," he said lightly.

"Trevor, how can you say such a thing? Celia might not wish to wear the necklace, but to say it was a favor to deprive her of anything so valuable. . . . Also, you must remember that the piece had a sentimental value to Lady Brompton."

"You are right, Aunt. I stand corrected." He bowed his head in acknowledgment of the reproof. "Celia, if I may be bold enough to call you that—"

"Of course you may do so, Trevor." The girl barely escaped giggling at her own temerity in calling a gentleman whom she had known for such a short time by his first name. Felicia thought that Ophelia Headly would certainly have done so under similar circumstances. Fortunately, either her parents or Lady Brompton had taught this child better manners.

"Then, Celia, I trust you will forgive and forget my foolish speech."

His contrite expression convinced the girl, but had no effect upon Felicia. He could charm this girl as he had charmed half the *ton* last evening at Almack's, but she alone knew him for the scoundrel he was. Aware of her thoughts, he threw her a mocking glance, as if daring her to expose him.

"Oh, I know you could never have meant it to be as heartless as it sounded," Celia assured him. "And, in one way, I suppose that you are right. Now that it is gone, I shall never be expected to wear it. But let us not talk more about this now. Everything has been said over and over, so I prefer to think of something more pleasant. I am certain Grandmama still plans to give a ball for me. Unhappy as she is about what happened, she will not allow it to change her plans. She said as much while you were there, did she not?"

"Yes," Felicia assured her. "She did say that. But it may be that this is not the best time . . ."

"If I beg her, she will do it, for she indulges me if she can do so. And it will give her something new to think about, which will be good for her. And you will come—all of you?"

Her glance was especially for Trevor, and Felicia told herself that she must warn Lady Brompton against him, if it did not prove that her ladyship could see through him for herself. Still, the old lady was quite sharp and doubtless could look after her granddaughter's welfare.

Further discussion of either the theft or Celia's ball was cut off when Hastings announced the arrival of Mr. Harrison. "I came as soon as I received your message," the young man said, bowing over Felicia's hand and raising it to his lips. "You cannot know how great was my disappointment at missing you earlier."

"As I explained in my message, sir, the news of Lady Brompton's loss drove all other thoughts from my mind. I am certain you can understand."

"Oh, certainly. You would have been concerned, as she is a friend. I had not meant to cavil about your absence, only to explain my disappointment."

"We had not meant to be from home for long, planning only to ask if we could be of help in any way, but she invited us in. We returned home to learn that we had missed your call."

"It is of no matter, now that you have allowed me to come. Although it is rather late, will you not accompany me for a ride in the Park? We shall still be in time to meet with a few members of the *ton*."

"It is kind of you to make such an offer, Mr. Harrison, but, as you can see, Holly has a guest at present, so is not free to accompany you at this afternoon."

Why must he have issued his invitation just at this time, rather at a time when she could have persuaded him that he should take Holly for a drive rather than herself? Being seen beside the young gentleman in the Park would have added to Holly's prestige.

"No—no. You misunderstand." The young man appeared rather ill at ease, smoothing his hair and tugging at his cravat until it was all askew.

Mr. Harrison had no great opinion of himself, despite the importance of his family background. Never had he considered himself to be a ladies' man and this sudden attachment to a lady of rather mature years was quite as surprising to him as it must be to anyone who knew him. "At the risk of sounding unforgivably rude to Miss Holly, it is not her company I wish—it is yours."

Without daring to look in Trevor's direction, Felicia could almost hear him saying, "Is that not what I told you?" She could feel the blood rising in her face. The man was completely incorrigible—Trevor, of course; James would never do anything to earn that description.

"You are most kind to offer to take me about, sir, but you can see that I cannot accept your invitation this afternoon. Even if Mr. Thomas is Holly's cousin, the relationship is not close enough for me to allow them to remain together without my presence. And since he is in no way related to Celia Burley, it would be most improper for me to leave them unchaperoned."

Trevor cleared his throat and half-rose. Felicia knew he was about to offer to take himself elsewhere, freeing her to accept the invitation, and shot him a dagger-glance. He grinned at her, but changed what he had been going to say, "All this might be solved quite easily, Mr. Harrison. Since your phaeton clearly will not hold all five of us, or even the three ladies and yourself, why do we not order out our carriage instead? In that way, no one of us need be left behind."

This was definitely not the sort of outing Mr. Harrison had in mind, but he was too much of a gentleman to tell the other that *his* company at such a time was unwelcome. So was that of the younger ladies, of course. Soon afterward, not quite certain how it had come about, he found himself seated beside the young Welshman in the Arsdale carriage, opposite Felicia, who had a young lady on either side of her.

Neither Holly nor Celia saw anything wrong with this arrangement and chattered happily across Felicia, in the manner of quite young ladies, each scarcely giving the other time to answer, and expecting none of the others to pay them the least attention. For his part, Trevor kept up a stream of light anecdotes which required replies from no one, but which gave Mr. Harrison time to wish that he had excused himself to go home and make his call on the fascinating Miss Arsdale at another time—preferably when her two charges were elsewhere.

Had he known it, Felicia was quite as miserable as he, although for a far different reason. She knew that Trevor was merely waiting until they were alone to taunt her with James Harrison's preference for her. And, much as she might try to convince him—and herself—that the young man was merely being polite to the relative of the young lady who really held his interest, she knew this to be untrue. Mr. Harrison had said as much this afternoon. Given time, of course, she could see that his attention was turned to Holly as it should be, but Trevor's presence made that more difficult.

Trevor's presence made *everything* more difficult, but she could see no way to rid herself of him until he had found the rich wife he sought, or until she had Holly safely married.

If she could not turn James Harrison's attention toward her sister, there were enough other eligible and wealthy gentlemen in London this Season. One of them might do very well as Holly's husband. It was only that James was so much more suitable in every way.

Late as it was, there were still enough people in the Park that they were stopped time after time to exchange greetings with acquaintances. Felicia suspected that some of those who halted beside their carriage were not truly acquaintances, but pretended the earlier meeting in order to be presented to Holly.

She greeted each of them with the same wide-eyed appearance of interest, then forgot them a moment later to continue her chattering to Celia. The other girl did not appear to mind the fact that she was virtually ignored by those who came to the carriage-side. Like a true, if recently acquired, friend, she rejoiced in Holly's popularity.

Having dismissed his own vehicle when the ride was suggested, Mr. Harrison had no choice but to accompany the party until they had left the environs of the Park, then he asked if he might be driven home. It was clear to him that Mr. Thomas, at least, was determined that he should have no time alone with the lady of his choice, although he could not understand the reason for this.

"Must you leave us so soon?" that gentleman asked. "It is not truly so late. We might have several more hours to drive about."

"No, Mr. Harrison has the right of it," Felicia told him. "We must let him go quite soon, and Celia, as well, for we are promised to Mrs. Armstrong's ball tonight, and the girls must have their rest, so that they will be able to enjoy themselves properly. Do we see you there, sir?" she asked.

"I have been asked, of course." A Harrison would be asked to every event of importance. "May I ask a dance with you?"

"You forget, Mr. Harrison, chaperons do not dance." It was said half regretfully, for Felicia had enjoyed the few opportunities she had for dancing; however, she would not have wished to dance with James. Unbidden, the memory of being whirled about the room in Trevor's embrace came to mind. She put it aside hurriedly; she did not wish *that*, either.

"Then I shall not dance."

The fervency of his statement gave Felicia the idea that he would do much to win her approval. She might use this to her, or rather to Holly's, advantage. Leaning toward him, she said, "But it would please me if you were to dance with my niece tonight."

"If you wish it, I shall do so." He bowed over the hand she had extended and would have kissed it, not seeing Trevor reaching backward to tug at the coachman's coat-tails. The man obediently drew his team to a sudden halt, with the result that James slid from the seat to his knees at Felicia's feet.

Giving no sign that he had expected something of the kind to happen, Trevor helped him up, inquiring solicitously if he had injured himself. The same sentiments were echoed more sincerely by Felicia, who proceeded to scold William for his thoughtless handling of his cattle and his lack of consideration for his passengers.

"But, Aunt, you would not have him run down an urchin in the street," Trevor protested, turning to wink at William, who took his cue at once, aware that Mr. Thomas would amply reward him for doing so.

"Right under the hooves, he was, miss," he said. "Then off so quick you could hardly see him."

"Then you certainly could do nothing else," Felicia said. She had not caught sight of any urchin, but, of course, she had, at that moment, been concentrating upon persuading James to dance with Holly. It *might* have happened as

William said, but for some reason she could not explain, she doubted that he was being entirely truthful about the matter. "But do try to drive more carefully in future. Have a thought for us, as well as for street children."

After James had been set down, promising to see them at the ball and also at Lady Carelton's Venetian breakfast next day, Felicia turned back to face Trevor angrily. "You did that purposely!"

"I?" The look he turned on her was innocence itself. "You heard William say that he was forced to pull up to avoid running down a street urchin."

"Yes, I heard what he said, after you had given him a hint. And I should like William to remember that he is *my* coachman, not yours."

A twitch of the servant's shoulders told that the shaft had struck its mark. Still, she did not doubt that he would continue to do whatever Trevor wished. If only there was some way that she could rid herself of this detestable young man.

"But—but, Miss Arsdale," Celia protested, wide-eyed, "you would not have wished him to harm a poor child." Holly nodded vigorous agreement.

"Certainly not," Felicia assured them. "Although I feel William might have handled the team more carefully had he tried to do so. Still, no real harm was done—to anyone." A sudden recollection of Mr. Harrison's expression when he was jolted to his knees before her made her bite her lips. It would not do to remind either of the young ladies of how ridiculous he had appeared.

Recovering her composure, she continued, "And now, my child, we must take up your maid and return you home without more delay, since I suppose that you plan on attending the Armstrong ball tonight—"

"I think we shall do so. Unless Grandmama decides that

she does not wish to face so many curious questions, and sends her regrets."

"If she prefers not to go, ask her to send us a message and you may go with us."

"Oh, that would be so kind of you, for I should dislike having to remain at home. The Season is so short and I should like to enjoy every moment of it, not sit at home. Will you wait a moment when we reach the house, and I can run in and ask what she wishes to do."

She smiled down at Trevor, who had alighted to give Celia's maid a hand into the carriage, an action which appeared to fluster that person, unaccustomed as she was to receiving any sort of consideration on the part of the upper orders.

"I think we might wait," the gentleman said. "Do you not agree, Aunt?"

"Certainly, we shall wait." Felicia was determined that she must warn Lady Brompton of Trevor's unsuitability for Celia. The girl was far too inexperienced to cope with such a rogue. Although how she was to say anything without giving away her own deception or allowing him to do so, she did not know.

Followed by her maid, who had somewhat recovered her sense of decorum, Celia ran up the steps to the front door, which was being held for her by one of the servants. She was within doors only a moment, then returned to say, "Thank you for the offer, Miss Arsdale—and T-Trevor— but Grandmama says that she feels much recovered and plans to attend the ball tonight—and if anyone asks about her necklace, she will tell them she did see the thief; he was seven feet tall and had green horns."

"Bravo for your grandmama," Trevor said and swung himself back into the carriage. He thought at first to take the place Celia had vacated, but caught Felicia's look and seated himself again with his back to the horses. "A doughty old lady," he commented.

"Yes, that describes her well. I have no doubt she *would* have thrown her candlestick at the thief if she had seen him, no matter how many others might say she would have been afraid to do so."

"If she had merely ordered him away, I am certain he would have gone quietly. Her ladyship is the sort who will always be obeyed."

Holly looked from one of them to the other. "Would it not have been dangerous for her ladyship to threaten some-one of that kind?"

"Doubtless it would have been, but I doubt that thought would have stopped her," Felicia said.

"And since she slept soundly throughout the theft, she was certainly in no danger," Trevor assured the younger girl. "I doubt the man wanted a scene—slipping out with the jewels would have been the wisest thing he could have done."

"Oh." Satisfied by his explanation, Holly returned her thoughts to a matter more important to her, the choice of a gown for tonight's ball. Felicia was happy to have the subject turned; although she could not fail to sympathize with Lady Brompton's loss, she considered that too much had already been said about it.

Although tonight's ball might not be as important in Holly's Season as her appearance at Almack's, Felicia made certain that the girl once more looked her best. After all, James Harrison had promised that he would dance with her, and Felicia hoped that would be enough to convince him that she was the girl he ought to choose.

Mrs. Armstrong preened herself as she bustled through her crowded room to greet Felicia and her "charges." Except for last evening's appearance at Almack's, *her* ball was the first to be graced by the presence of the handsome Mr. Thomas.

Her fond hope was that his eye might be taken by one of her three daughters, the eldest being already in her third Season without having received a single offer and the others now having reached marriageable age, as well. Not even the most optimistic of mamas could think that any of them could compare with Holly Arsdale's beauty—but, since the Beauty was his cousin, it was probable that he was uninterested in that line, but was merely escorting her and his aunt out of kindness.

Holly was radiant in her gown of white muslin with the embroidery of silver acorns, having observed last evening that the depth of its neckline, about which she had been worried, was actually quite modest in comparison with the gowns of many of the other young ladies. Some of them, she had thought, were quite shockingly low, so she was able to restrain herself from tugging at hers, as she had tried to do when she first donned it.

Almost at once, Felicia surrendered her to James Harrison for the promised dance, hoping that he would be kept so occupied during the remainder of the evening that he would have no time to approach her. Trevor escorted his "aunt" toward the chaperon's corner where she was hailed at once by Lady Brompton. "Come and sit by me," the old lady commanded. "I know I need not be expected to answer any number of stupid questions from you."

She was wearing as many jewels as before, including a diamond necklace of some magnificence. "Doubtless her second best," Trevor said in a low tone, making Felicia bite her lips. Why must he always tempt her to laughter at the most inopportune moments?

She shot him a quelling glance, which he ignored, and took the place indicated, saying with a laugh, "No, since I have already asked them all," as she looked about her with interest.

She had thought that Almack's, despite its importance to the *ton*, was a drab place. Certainly, nothing had been done to make the room decorative, and Felicia had noted that many dancers had trouble upon the uneven floor. The decor of Almack's, like the refreshments it offered, was not designed to detract from the importance of its favored members.

Mrs. Armstrong had gone to the other extreme in decorating her ballroom. Swaths of pink silk billowed across the ceiling and down the walls, covering even the windows and giving the room the appearance of an enormous tent.

Between a forest of potted palm trees, numerous mirrors, each surrounded by garlands of flowers, reflected the dancers, the glitter of hundreds of candles and the twinkling prisms of the large chandeliers, as well as the urns and statues that stood along the wall wherever there was a bit of space for them. Many of the statues had been draped in yards of the pink silk, doubtless to hide their unclothed state from those who might be shocked by their appearance.

Brushing aside a drooping palm frond which had been tickling her neck—and, she feared, disarranging her wig—Felicia glanced toward Lady Brompton, who leaned forward, but hardly troubled to lower her voice as she said, "Quite right, my dear, it is an excessively vulgar display. But what can one expect from a woman who wears rubies with a puce gown, or who decorates her daughters as if they were Maypoles?"

She nodded toward a trio across the room, who had clearly been dressed by the hand which had decorated the room, for their gowns, although originally white—even that of the eldest girl—had been so covered with bows and floss that the color was not visible, and their hair had been

crimped and frizzed until it almost seemed they were
wearing wigs. All of them had inherited their mother's
robust form and, although none could be called beautiful,
they would have been more attractive in simple gowns and
coiffures, rather than looking like grotesque dolls, as they
now did.

"Oh, dear," Felicia could think of nothing else to say, but
the older lady nodded knowingly.

"Exactly. They are far from being frights when allowed
to dress simply. The trouble is their mother has a free hand
with the purse, and not an ounce of brains to accompany it."

The dance was ending and Felicia saw her sister being
handed to another partner, her popularity again being so
great that she was seldom returned to her "aunt's" care
between sets, as should have been done. Since the Lady
Patronesses had not objected to such behavior last evening,
it was not likely that anyone would look askance at the same
taking place on this occasion.

Felicia braced herself as she saw James Harrison coming
in her direction, but he was skillfully intercepted by Mrs.
Armstrong. No matter how carefully a hostess might plan
these affairs, there were always many more young ladies
than gentlemen in attendance, and such an important young
man could not be permitted to waste his time among the
dowagers.

To her credit, she did not lead him at once to her
daughters, but presented him to a shy young lady who
accepted his partnership gratefully. Felicia drew a deep
breath and silently forgave Mrs. Armstrong her crudities for
keeping the young gentleman from her side. She did not
doubt the hostess would keep a sharp eye upon James for
the remainder of the evening, and see that he was not
without partners.

Ophelia Headly scurried up to them, followed at a more
sedate pace by Celia Burley. "Is it not the most exciting

thing you have ever heard?" Ophelia demanded, between her customary giggles.

"How can you say it is exciting? I think it is rather dreadful," Celia objected.

Ophelia, however, was quite as difficult to turn aside from a subject which interested her as her mother would have been. "Oh, no, if only someone would be willing to fight a duel over *me*, I think I might *die* from the excitement."

"In that case, the duel would be wasted, would it not?" Felicia commented, recalling that Ophelia had also thought she would die if she found a thief in her bedchamber. It appeared to be the young lady's favorite mode of expression. "What duel do you mean?" She hoped no one was fighting over Holly; that would be scandalous.

"Oh, Mr. Atwood challenged Lord Apley because he— Mr. Atwood, I mean—said that his lordship had slighted Lucy Main in some way. I do not know how—no one would give us the details. It must have been something quite shocking, I suppose." This premise evoked another giggle. "At any rate, they are to fight at dawn tomorrow."

"I still think it is terrible," Celia declared. "And, anyway, duels are illegal. Are they not?" she asked her grandmother.

"I believe they are, although one hears that they do still take place at times. Did not the Duke of Wellington take part in one, or does my memory play me false?"

"I—I am not certain," replied Felicia, since the query appeared to be addressed to her.

Lady Brompton shrugged. "It does not matter. But whatever the outcome of the affair, the girl will be ruined. Not even marriage to the winner will be enough to make her acceptable. It is not like it was when I was young, when a lady's name might be protected in such a way."

"Oh, I think you are horrid, Celia, not to see how

wonderful it would be to have someone wanting to fight over you. Not that anyone would ever wish to do so." With this parting shot, Ophelia marched away.

"Her mother's daughter in every way," Lady Brompton commented. "And I should not worry about what she says, Celia."

"Oh, I do not, she is so foolish, wanting someone to fight over her, as if anyone would do so, which is what she said about me, is it not?" She laughed, but was immediately serious again. "She does not think that a man might be killed. Or perhaps she would like that too. It is all so senseless."

She moved away on the arm of her next partner, as Felicia watched Trevor lead one Miss Armstrong onto the floor, and told herself that she could not warn every mama against allowing her charge to become interested in the scoundrel. And why should she do so in this case? She did not doubt that Mrs. Armstrong could well endow any of her daughters; had not Lady Brompton said she had a free hand with her purse?

A dowry of sufficient size could do much to improve the young lady's appearance. And, after all, the sooner Trevor found the wealthy wife he wanted, the sooner he would be out of her life, and she could be free to concentrate on getting Holly married.

Of course, James Harrison would not ask Holly to dance a second time. That would have been seen as a declaration of his intentions toward her, and, much as Felicia might wish it, she knew he had no such intentions.

Yet.

Ignoring the many curious glances at her uncovered head—uncovered except for her wig—for she knew this would be dismissed as merely another eccentricity, such as her insistence upon being addressed as Miss Arsdale, she spent the evening happily comparing notes about various other guests with Lady Brompton. Despite the great difference in their ages, she found the old lady more to her liking than many of the younger members of the *ton*.

There was a stir as a newcomer entered the room. Mrs. Armstrong's massive bosom fairly heaved with pride at having such an important guest at her affair. He had been invited, of course, as he was invited everywhere, but she had hardly expected that he would come. He was known to be quite selective about the affairs he attended, and seldom accepted invitations unless there was something beyond the ordinary to pique his interest.

As she moved forward to greet him, however, the young gentleman ignored her and approached the crowd about Holly, which parted as if on unspoken command. Each of the others covertly inspected his own attire, as if expecting to receive a setdown, but the newcomer ignored them, as well, having eyes only for Holly. Eager as the others had been for her company, there was not so much as a raised eyebrow among them when he drew her out onto the floor, tucked her hand beneath his arm and led her to Felicia's chair.

"Miss Arsdale, I beg the honor of your niece's company for a dance."

Despite the fact that his behavior in coming to ask her permission was better than that shown by many of the gentlemen here tonight, Felicia was about to refuse her consent, but a sharp nudge from the old lady at her side caused her to nod assent. The pair moved onto the floor, his arm about Holly for the waltz.

"Who in the world is that?" Felicia wanted to know, wondering why her ladyship had been so insistent that she permit the dance.

Lady Brompton chuckled. "Only the arbiter of fashion in London. The one man even the prince will heed, at times, but not often enough, more's the pity."

"He? But he is dressed so plainly, not a touch of color about him."

"No, he has decreed that only black—with a white cravat, carefully tied—is the proper evening wear for a gentleman of the *ton*. And no jewelry, of course. Have you not seen how many ape his style? None of them can handle himself, however, with such panache. That, my dear, is the celebrated Beau Brummell."

Felicia stared. She had heard of the Beau, of course. But this rather small man certainly had nothing about him to attract one's attention. He would easily be overlooked in a crowd, except that the crowd appeared to wait upon his praise or criticism.

The waltz had ended and Mr. Brummell returned Holly to Felicia's side, raising her hand to his lips before she was quickly claimed by another gentlemen. It was not the custom for a gentleman to kiss the hand of a young, unmarried lady, but Mr. Brummell did not concern himself with following customs. Rather, he set them. With a bow to Felicia and another sketched vaguely in the direction of his approaching hostess, but with no word of farewell, the Beau turned and left the ballroom.

"How odd," Felicia commented. "To arrive here, dance only once, then leave."

"Yes, but you do not understand what a compliment he has paid your niece. Doubtless, he had heard of her, so was impelled to see her for himself, since he was absent from Almack's last evening. Not that she was in need of it, I must own, but his approval has given your little Beauty an additional renown. A renown that many of this Season's debutante's would give theirs souls to obtain. Her success is assured."

"And if he had not approved of her?"

Her ladyship shook her head sadly. "That would have

been a bad thing. I do not know whether even your Holly's beauty would have been enough to overcome it."

"I see." But she hardly did so. Could anyone truly have so much power? Because the approval of this one little man meant so much to the *ton*, however, she was grateful that he had shown his approval of Holly. It should make her task so much easier.

If James did not approach Holly a second time, there were a number of young gentlemen who did so, many of them induced as much by the Beau's approval as by the girl's own beauty. Holly, however, was able to remember that she was not to stand up more than once in an evening with any gentleman.

Those unable to dance with her insisted upon bringing her cup after cup of Mrs. Armstrong's lemonade, which she thought had no more flavor than the orgeat she had drunk last evening at Almack's, but which she did not know how to refuse.

Trevor saw her dilemma and came quickly to her side. "Now, how can you expect one little lady to drink all of that?" he asked. "I suggest that each of you drink your own."

"Drink *this*?" one of them asked, horrified. "Myself? You cannot mean what you say, sir. This is no drink for a man."

"Nor for a lady, I should say," Trevor said. He offered his arm to Holly and led her back to Felicia. "The crowd there," he gestured over his shoulder, "plans to drown our Holly, it seems to me."

"And to me," Holly agreed. "I do not know why all of them seem to think I should like to drink so much. Truly, it does not taste so good."

"It is merely their way of attempting to make you keep them in mind, since they know that you cannot dance with them again tonight," Felicia told her, not liking the manner in which Trevor referred to the girl as "our Holly." However, that was merely part of his performance as Holly's cousin, so she could say nothing about it. "And have you enjoyed your dancing, Holly?"

"Oh, yes, even my dance with that odd-looking young gentleman. He did dance very well, but he looked so queer, dressed as he was."

"Do not allow anyone to hear you speak in such a way of the great Beau Brummell," Trevor told her. "His approval or disapproval of a lady means as much as that of the Prince Regent."

"Brummell would doubtless say that it counted for much more," Lady Brompton told them. "And he may well be right about the matter."

"I see, but I think——" Holly yawned widely. It was fortunate, Felicia thought, that her back was to the crowd of admirers. Else they might have thought she was bored by their attentions, which could be fatal to her chances. Why could she not teach the girl to simulate pleasure in such company, even when she did not feel it?

Before Holly could commit some other *faux pas*, Felicia said hurriedly, "Perhaps, then, it is time for us to say good night. We can send the carriage back for you, Trevor. There is no need for you to leave." Let him stay; perhaps he could fix his interest with one of the wealthy young ladies of the house. It was certain that their hostess would have no objections to a speedy courtship.

"Certainly not. I should not think of allowing you to go alone," he told her, taking her arm as well as Holly's and frowning away several young gentlemen who had planned to beg a dance with the Incomparable.

At home, he bade them a good night and mounted at once to his room. Felicia saw Holly into Evans's capable hands and retired to her own room. She had not thought that her role as chaperon would be such a fatiguing one, but her

efforts to interest James Harrison in Holly were more
wearying than she realized. Although she had thought to
begin her guest list for Holly's ball, she was asleep almost
as soon as she climbed into her bed.

She half-roused at the sound of footsteps passing her
door, then came fully awake as the front door closed. Who
could be wandering about at this hour, she asked herself,
but reason told her it could be no one but Trevor.

"So he had not been as weary as he pretended," she said
to herself, "and is slipping out for some purpose of his
own." An assignation, perhaps, but then, why should he not
go where he pleased, as long as he did not interfere with her
plans? And why should he tell her what he meant to do?
Certainly, she was not his guardian. Thankful for that, she
burrowed her head in her pillow and returned to slumber.

Whether it was because Mrs. Headly did not believe that
Mrs. Armstrong's affairs were worth reporting, or whether
she was still angry because Felicia had not taken her to Lady
Brompton's the day before, it was not until the three of them
arrived at Lady Carelton's breakfast that they heard the
dreadful news.

In the night, a thief had entered Mrs. Armstrong's
bedchamber, just as he had done at Lady Brompton's. Once
more he had been able to slip into the room and leave again
without wakening the occupant. But this time, he had not
been content with a single item, but taken all her jewels.

# * Six *

LADY CARELTON MIGHT consider either that her Venetian breakfast was a success or a fiasco, depending upon her viewpoint. True, the weather was exceptionally fine, so that her guests need not huddle indoors, but might stroll among the early roses or seek out the secluded nooks of her garden if they so desired.

Her spacious lawns were crowded with enough people to please any hostess' heart. They devoured the delicacies for which her chef was famous and kept her army of servants running to replenish emptied glasses as they strolled about, talking to one another.

However, even the flirtations and surreptitious meetings which were always to be expected at such an event took second place today to the far more interesting gossip. A small group of the people were discussing the duel, which had taken place that morning, regardless of the ban that had been placed on duelling.

Having had time to think more coolly about what he was going to do and to consider whether further compromising the young lady's name, which he had quite unintentionally slandered, was worth the possibility of having a hole blown through him, Lord Apley had fired into the air, and everyone expected that Mr. Atwood would be honorable enough to do the same.

Mr. Atwood, however, had aimed directly at his opponent and had only missed registering a fatal shot because of the poor marksmanship he had not taken into consideration when he issued the challenge. He had clipped a large piece out of Lord Apley's left sleeve, giving his lordship reason to complain about the ruin of his good coat, and giving his friends the opportunity to say that Mr. Atwood had behaved like a poor sport and should be cut.

The fact that he had no way of knowing in advance what his opponent was going to do was ignored by everyone, even by his second. Since he was the man who was supposed to be duelling in defense of Miss Main's good name, it suffered badly as a consequence, and the girl's angry parents had packed her off to a great-aunt in Bath before the morning was over.

Even this interesting event, however, was overlooked by most of the guests, who could talk about nothing except the latest theft. The daring of the man who had invaded two well-known houses on successive nights was applauded by a few, most of the sporting gentlemen, but deplored by the greater number of the guests. Who knew where the villain might strike next?

"I own that I considered her rubies in the worst of taste," Lady Brompton said privately to Felicia. "Especially since she *would* wear them with whatever she might have donned, even a walking dress. And that they would be well lost, despite the fact that they must be worth a fortune. Let us hope she replaces them with some more tasteful gems, although I doubt she will do so. But to praise the man who stole them, certainly the same one who took my diamond necklace, is outside of enough."

"I agree with you wholeheartedly. Although my—my nephew, Trevor, is among those who see the thief's exploits as admirable. Not," she hastened to add, lest anyone leap to the wrong conclusion as to the reason for his admiration;

much as she disliked the man herself, she could not permit anyone to think her relative the sort who would condone a crime, "that I believe he considers that the theft itself was admirable, but merely thinks that anyone who takes such chances deserves a sort of respect."

"I am certain he does not admire the theft itself. The young man has more sensibility than that, and can feel for those of us who had lost our valuables. But you realize, my dear Felicia, that young men—especially those young gentlemen whose lives have been somewhat restricted by the rules of the *ton*—are quite apt to see such acts as those of a modern-day Robin Hood, stealing only from those who can well afford the loss. Although I doubt if many of the gains will ever go to help the poor."

But Trevor is not so young as that, Felicia said to herself. And I doubt the rogue has led a restricted life. Unbidden came the memory of his slipping out of the house last night as easily as he had slipped within on the day she had first seen him.

She pushed the thought aside, however, as unworthy of consideration. A reprehensible creature the man certainly was, and a blackmailer who was forcing her to sponsor him in the *ton*, but *surely* he was no thief. A man whose wish was to find a wealthy wife would scarcely risk his opportunities in that line by committing thefts in which he could well be apprehended.

"I suppose you are right," she said to Lady Brompton, "but I must own that I dislike hearing him express such thoughts because he could well be misunderstood, and have told him as much. Not that he gives much care to my opinion."

"On the contrary, it is clear that he must care very much for your good opinion. Not every young man who is on his first visit to London would care to take on the duty of escorting an aunt and a cousin about to these affairs. Most of them would prefer, I should think, to be spending their time gaming at White's or frequenting one of those awful boxing saloons where a man could show off his prowess. Or even pursuing some Cyprian or other, rather than dancing attendance upon members of his family."

"Yes." Felicia forced a smile she was far from feeling. "I must agree that Trevor is being very attentive to our welfare." The old lady could not know Trevor danced attendance upon her in the hope she would provide him the opportunity to gain a wealthy wife.

"You should value him for that, my dear," Lady Brompton advised, patting Felicia's hand. "Now, I had best see where Celia has wandered. There are too many rogues here who might wish to lure her into one of those secluded corners. And I doubt she has the good sense to refuse, especially if one hints that he wishes to speak of this morning's duel."

"But that would not happen, surely. Celia deplores the idea of duelling. Do you not recall how Ophelia Headly named her a spoilsport for not wishing someone to duel over her?"

"True enough, but when the duel has actually taken place without anyone being injured, the talk which has been going about—especially the scandal involving the gel involved— may well be enough to entice a young girl into some corner to listen to the tale."

"You are right, and I must see to Holly." She, also, would be amenable to almost any suggestion, not recognizing such a clandestine meeting as a threat to her reputation, if not to her virtue.

Felicia doubted that her sister would be lured by any talk of duelling, for she had a great dislike of anything violent. Still, one could never be certain of what she might be feeling, and she could be expected to listen with apparent interest to any tale a gentleman might tell, even if she did not understand a word of it. "When I saw her last, she was near that fountain between the trees, but she has gone elsewhere."

She walked to the fountain, which represented a pair of entwined—and unclad—lovers who were seated upon the back of some creature which vaguely resembled a dolphin. Felicia wondered idly why anyone should have chosen so inauspicious a spot for a tryst, but dismissed the subject as due to the vagaries of the supposed artist.

Holly was no longer in sight; Felicia looked about her in all directions, but before she could find any sign of the girl, she saw James Harrison apparently heading toward the fountain. Hoping that she might remain unseen, she stepped back quietly, caught a heel upon the low stone ledge about the fountain, and felt herself falling backward.

A strong arm about her waist prevented her from tumbling into the water. She twisted about to look up so that she might thank her rescuer and gasped to find Trevor's face so near her own. "What are you doing here?" she demanded.

"If you mean, what am I doing at this gathering, you must remember that I was the one who escorted you and Holly to this affair. If you mean in this spot, I *thought* I was saving you from a wetting, but if you prefer that to my company . . ."

She felt the arm loosen about her and, still off balance, was forced to grasp at his coat to prevent herself from falling. "No, no, I did not mean that, of course. I was merely startled to see you here at the moment, for I had not known you were near. I am thankful that you saved me from taking a spill into the fountain. It would be most uncomfortable to go about for the remainder of the afternoon with my clothing soaked."

"There are many here who might welcome the excuse to appear in such a way, but I am certain you are not among them. Not to mention, of course, what such a soaking might do to your hair," he said in a low tone. Then, as if he had only now become aware of the young man who was walking about near them, he called, "Ah, Mr. Harrison. Were you looking for us?"

"Yes—that is—no." James was far too much a gentleman to say that he wished Mr. Thomas were elsewhere; certainly, he was far from pleased to see him apparently embracing Miss Arsdale. After all, the fellow might be her nephew, but that gave him no liberty to behave toward her as he was doing.

If others besides himself had seen them, there might be talk. And he wanted no such talk about Miss Arsdale. Not that he would go so far as to challenge the fellow to a duel, as Atwood had done last evening; there must be any number of better ways of ridding oneself of an unwanted relative of his lady.

He wondered briefly if his father might be amenable to forcing the other man to go abroad—perhaps to Jamaica— but decided that the earl would do little to aid him in his present suit. Cranston and his son seldom saw eye-to-eye on any subject, and James doubted they would do so on the subject of Felicia Arsdale.

Well aware of the thoughts going through the other's mind, excepting the part about the possibility of sending him to Jamaica, Trevor set Felicia firmly upon both feet beside the fountain, inquiring with false solicitude, "And are you certain that you are feeling quite the thing now, Aunt? Doubtless, all of this excitement about duels and thefts has been responsible for oversetting you."

Nothing oversets me so much as your presence, Felicia thought, but said, "Y-yes, thank you, Trevor. I am quite well now."

"Then, it might be a good thing for me to run and fetch you a glass of negus. I should be able to find something of the kind among the plentitude of potables available. It should strengthen you. I am certain that I leave you in good hands."

"No, no, you need not bring it. Truly, I need nothing." Felicia was in a quandry. She did not wish for Trevor's presence, but even less did she wish to be left alone with James Harrison. "I must make haste; I was on my way to find where Holly had gone."

"Do not trouble yourself about my cousin. She is not the sort to fall into mischief, I am certain. I shall find her for you and bring her to you later—much later," he added so softly that only she could hear the last word. She could not see his face since he had already turned away, but was certain he was wearing the mocking grin which greeted most of her efforts to rid herself of him.

Barely waiting until the other man was out of hearing, James Harrison began, "My lady—"

"Please, I beg of you not to call me that. I am merely *Miss* Felicia Arsdale." She spoke sharply, ill at ease, for she knew he was about to make some flowery speech, and she did not wish to hear it. Still, aside from being rude enough to walk away, there was no way to prevent him from saying whatever was uppermost on his mind.

"But permit me to go on thinking of you as my lady, which you know I do." His tone was so ardent that she devoutly hoped that no one was within listening distance. "I must speak to you, but not here, where we might be interrupted at any time." Especially by your infernal nephew, he added to himself. "May I call upon you tomorrow morning?"

She swallowed a sigh of relief. At least, she would have more time to prepare herself to listen to him. And possibly to work out some scheme to turn his interest from herself to Holly. "I—I cannot say anything at the moment, for I scarcely know what plans Holly may have for the morning."

At the thought of still another encumbrance to Miss Arsdale's time, he forgot himself and uttered a rude word. Felicia gave him a reproachful look, and James was immediately contrite.

"I had not meant to speak in such a fashion before you, but you must know that I care not at all what plans Miss Holly might have. Or Mr. Thomas, either. Except that they might involve you. It is *you* I wish to visit tomorrow. I beg that you will forgive my boorishness—unforgivable as it is—and tell me I may do so."

She wished she might tell him that he was *not* welcome to call, but she felt that he would insist, and she could not quarrel with him here. Nor could she put an end to any chance for Holly's future by angering him.

If he persisted in his mad pursuit of her, she could definitely put an end to *that* when he called on the morrow. Somehow, she *must* turn his thoughts toward Holly. It was Holly who needed a husband, not she. And soon, so that she could tell Trevor Thomas to return to wherever he had been before he burst into their lives.

"Very well," she said at last, seeing no other way out of her dilemma, "I shall arrange to be at home tomorrow. Shall we say at eleven o'clock?"

"That would be excellent. And may I hope that you will be alone?"

"Really, Mr. Harrison, I am certain you must know that any such behavior as entertaining a gentleman alone is not permitted, even when one has reached my age." She hoped her show of indignation was enough to cover her unease at the thought of being alone with him.

"Yes, my la—my dear Miss Arsdale, I realize that my conduct would be reprehensible, under other conditions. But since you have no parent or guardian to whom I may tender my application, I am left with no choice but to speak to you directly. And I cannot do so before others, such as your niece and nephew. Until tomorrow, then." He caught her hand, raised it to his lips, and turned away just as Trevor reappeared, carrying a glass.

"Where is Holly?" she demanded.

"I said I should bring her to you later. Here is your negus, Aunt. And I trust your meeting was a satisfactory one."

Felicia snatched the glass from his hand and downed its contents in a single swallow, although she abhorred the warm drink. At the moment, she felt she would have preferred to have something much stronger—hartshorn and water, perhaps—or preferably a large dose of laudanum. One that was large enough to put her to sleep until after tomorrow morning.

Seeing her expression, Trevor said, "Was your talk truly so bad as all that?" For a moment, she thought she had detected a note of sympathy in his voice. Sympathy from her "devoted nephew"? How could she even have imagined anything of the sort?

"He is calling upon me tomorrow morning; he wishes to speak to me about Holly, of course. This may be what I have been wanting to hear."

Trevor looked at her for a moment, then shook his head. If she had imagined sympathy from him an instant ago, she knew how wrong she had been when he said, "You lie so poorly, Auntie dear, that I shall never know why you ever thought you could become a successful masquerader. I have told you, and I shall tell you again. The man is not even slightly interested in your birdwitted charge. Nor will he ever be, despite all your efforts in that direction. It is you he wants."

"Where did you go when you left the house last night?" she demanded, angered both by his ridiculing her troubles—most of which would not exist if it were not for him—and his uncalled-for description of her sister. It was true that Holly was far from being brilliant, but what affair was that of Trevor's?

She had not intended to permit him to know she was aware of his going, and she had no wish to begin an argument with him among all these people. Now, however, she was too angry at him to care if he knew.

"I? Last night? What gives you the idea that I left the house?"

The innocent look in his wide blue eyes did not deceive her for an instant. She had seen it frequently and knew it for fraud. "I know you went out because I heard you close the outer door."

"I was not aware that you were so interested in my comings and goings, Aunt." There was amusement in his tone, which angered her further.

If only there were not people nearby, she would have taken pleasure in telling him precisely what she thought of him. Under the present conditions, all she could say was, "I am *not* interested in what you do. It was only the surreptitious manner in which you left the house that came to my notice."

"That is true—I was attempting to keep my going quiet. But it was only because I did not wish to disturb your rest, not for any desire to deceive you. There are a number of places throughout the city, you must be aware, where a man might go without the females of his family accompanying him."

"I have no doubt of that."

The sarcasm in her tone only made him grin. "Some of them are quite unexceptional, I assure you. I might go to Cribb's Parlour, for example, to blow a cloud with some of my friends, except that I do not smoke. Or to Whites or Brooks's in order to place a wager. I do own to wagering from time to time, but not to the extent of some gentlemen. On the other hand—" he hesitated, as if unwilling to name some of the low places that catered to the tastes of certain gentlemen.

Felicia could feel her color rising, aware that he was taunting her again. "It is certainly no affair of mine," she said hastily, "where you might go or what you might choose to do. As long as you do nothing to harm Holly's chance with the *ton*."

"You may rest assured, my dear Auntie," he said solemnly, "that I shall do nothing at all to reflect badly upon the Arsdale name. Now, have you and Holly had enough of this melee which calls itself a breakfast, or do you plan to remain longer?"

"I think it best that we should leave soon. I see that a number of our friends have gone and we should certainly not be among the last to go. I must find Holly and bid adieu to our hostess."

"As you wish, of course. I should suggest, however, that you straighten your wig before someone notices it and begins to wonder that some of your hair is suddenly of a different color than the rest. It seems that you have set it somewhat askew—doubtless in your perturbation about your young suitor."

It was more probable that it had been disturbed when she tripped and Trevor had caught her. She wondered that James had not noticed the varied colors. "Not my suitor, as I have told you—and I should advise you to attend to your own affairs and leave me to mine." Wrenching her wig about until it covered her hair properly, she stalked off on her errands.

Finding Holly was a simple matter, after all, for she was surrounded by the usual great number of admirers, each of them thinking her wide-eyed stare was a sign of deep interest in his speech. Lady Carelton, however, was nowhere to be seen.

As a member of the *ton*, her ladyship felt it necessary for her to arrange such amusements for her friends, but she seldom attended them herself. Having assured herself that the necessary crush of guests had accepted her invitation to impress everyone with her success as a hostess, she had retired to her bed for a midafternoon rest with a novel and a box of bonbons, leaving the task of serving the crowd to her well-organized staff. The people between the pages of her novel she found far more interesting than those upon her lawn.

When she had been assured by the servants that her ladyship was not to be seen at the moment, Felicia reluctantly removed her sister from her clutch of young gentlemen. It might be, she told herself, that she would have to choose one among them for Holly, if Mr. Harrison persisted in his attentions to herself. However, she felt unwilling to think that any of such Dandies as these would be the right man for Holly, and she was still certain that she could convince James that the young Incomparable would be the perfect wife for him.

"We shall not need the carriage tonight, William," Felicia told the coachman as they alit before the house.

"You have made no plans for the evening?" Trevor asked, being fully aware of the large number of invitations that were arriving at the house each day. Between the numerous hostesses who visualized Holly as the right wife for one of their sons, and the ones who saw Trevor as the perfect mate for one of this year's debutantes, the greatest task for Felicia was to choose which of the functions to attend.

"No, I think it best that Holly have a quiet evening, for I am certain she found the al fresco breakfast quite fatiguing. I did too."

"That is good," Holly said. "I am so weary at the moment that I truly think I should fall asleep on my feet if I were forced to dance tonight."

"Oh, that must never happen, so we must see that you have the proper rest."

"Then you will not require my escort?"

"Thank you, no, Trevor." No matter what she might feel, she was always polite to him in public. "However, I ought not to have dismissed William without asking your plans for tonight. If you wish to use the carriage, feel free—"

"I think not, although it is good of you to offer me its use. I shall probably go out, but the carriage will not be needed."

"Where shall you go, Trevor?" Holly wanted to know.

"Curiosity must be a family trait," he said with a laugh. "Or is it merely that it is a female one?"

"What does that mean?" The effort to puzzle out his words caused her to frown, making Felicia uneasy. The smallest line would be ruinous to Holly's incomparable beauty.

"It means that he does not intend to tell us, Holly." She tugged at her sister's arm, drawing her into the house. "Doubtless he plans to attend some disreputable affair," she explained in a low tone, causing Holly to stare wide-eyed at her "cousin," who merely laughed.

"Aunt Felicia is quite right—these are not the places a young lady should know about."

"Oh." The other two wondered if Holly had the least idea of what he had meant.

Felicia said, "Then, if you do not wish the carriage, I suppose we shall not see you until the morning. Or will you be at home for dinner?"

"I think not. Some friends have suggested a late dinner, and perhaps a game afterward. So I shall bid you a good night now."

Happy to be free of him, at least for the evening, Felicia prepared to give orders to have a light repast for herself and Holly, when Hastings presented her with a message which had come from Lady Brompton.

"I realize that this is in a way an imposition, to invite you upon such short notice. However, Celia has been badgering me for several days to take her to the theater to see Edmund Kean as Macbeth, although why she should wish to see anything so violent, I cannot understand. But, as usual, I shall allow her to have her way, and a night at the theater will be more restful for her than one spent in dancing.

"I have a box at Drury Lane, of course. If you and your two charges would like to accompany us, we might go there this evening. I should find such an outing much more enjoyable with your company, and Celia is fond of Holly. Please inform me as to whether your nephew will be willing to escort you. If not, I can send my carriage to bring you to us."

No one except Lady Brompton would issue an invitation with so little warning as this and expect that it would be accepted. Had any other presumed to send such a message, Felicia would have consigned it to the fireplace without a second thought and without sending an answer. She liked the old lady, however, and was reluctant to refuse to do what she asked.

"What do you think, Holly?" Felicia asked. "Should you enjoy an evening at the theater?"

"Perhaps, since we have never been, I cannot tell what it might be like. But at least, I should be able to sit down, and not have to dance time after time."

"Good. Then we shall plan on going. She invites Trevor as well, but I think he will prefer to meet with his cronies."

Still, she sent a message to his room, telling what Lady Brompton had requested. Trevor came down to her at once.

"I do not wish to overset your plans for the evening," Felicia said. "After all, her ladyship has offered to send her carriage for us, so your escort will not be needed, if you prefer to meet your friends. However, since she has suggested your company, I thought you should be told about our plans."

"Of course I should prefer to go with you. Like you, I always enjoy her ladyship's company, and I have heard that Kean is a superb actor. This may be my only opportunity of seeing him—at least, in such company. I shall merely send a message to my friends, suggesting that we have a late supper instead. It will not matter to them. Shall I tell William he will be needed after all?"

"Yes, I think it best to have him take us to the theater, rather than imposing upon Lady Brompton. I shall tell her we accept; then we must change at once, although I am not certain what one wears to the theater. One of our ball gowns, I suppose. The *ton* may consider it fashionable to be late in arriving at the theater, but I am certain Lady Brompton does not subscribe to that idea."

Word was sent to the kitchen to have a light dinner served at once. "Cold meats will be quite sufficient," the cook was told. Nonetheless, she hastened to whip together what she considered proper to be served to such important persons as her mistress and the two younger people. They were forced to eat in some haste, lest they arrive late, after all.

"My dear Felicia, it was so kind of you to come to us upon such short notice," Lady Brompton said when they arrived at the theater.

"Not at all; you are presenting us with quite a treat. We have not yet attended the theater, so are eagerly awaiting the performance."

"And how many hostesses will you disappoint tonight by not gracing their balls?"

"None, as far as Holly and I are concerned. We had not planned on going out tonight. Holly feels that she has had enough dancing for a night or two. As for Trevor, I believe he meant to spend some time with friends, attending clubs

or something of the sort. Not what the females of his family
should know about, he implied."

"But nothing I could not omit gladly in order to accept
your kind invitation," Trevor said gallantly, bowing over
the old lady's hand.

She struck his arm with her fan, as flirtatious as any
young girl. The handsome Welshman had quickly become a
favorite of hers.

"Then we shall have a happy evening," she said, as she
allowed him to take her wrap and arrange her chair for the
best view of both the stage and the audience. Trevor would
then have performed the same service for Felicia, but she
had already seated herself, while the younger ladies began
chattering together in their customary way.

The theater was lavishly decorated with marble and gilt,
the chairs with gilded backs and velvet cushions. The front
of each box displaying a garland with a medallion in its
center. Since the building was only a few years old, its
decorations had not had time to become tawdry, although
smoke from the footlights had darkened parts of the
curtains.

"I am happy that we arrived before the performance
began," Lady Brompton said, scanning the other boxes to
see if anyone of importance might be attending. Felicia did
the same, although she knew there were many people whom
she had not met.

"Who is that lady over there?" Holly asked. "The one in
the gown with all the feathers?"

# * Seven *

CELIA GIGGLED AND poked her friend, attempting to hush her, but Lady Brompton declared, "Your upbringing leaves much to be desired, Celia, if you recognize that person. At least, you should have the good taste to pretend that you do not."

"Well, who is she?" Holly persisted, much puzzled by the reaction to her question.

"She is not a lady, of that you may be certain." Lady Brompton had put up her lorgnette to observe the female in the box across from them. "That is Harriette Wilson with her latest conquest, and one of her sisters accompanies her, I believe, although I cannot be certain of that. The other three are not quite so notorious, or so easily recognized as she."

"But who is she?"

"Shush." That was Celia, poking her again. "No one talks about her."

"That is not entirely true, Miss Celia. Everyone talks about her," Trevor corrected. "Only not in front of nice ladies such as the two of you."

Holly still looked bewildered, so Felicia put a hand on her arm to comfort her. She was aware of Holly's discomfort at being unable to understand what her friend and her "cousin" meant. "Let us merely say that she is not at all a nice person. One that we should not wish to know. Although I must own that I am surprised that she should be here."

"Oh, the Wilson sisters may be seen everywhere," her ladyship declared. "Why should they not? They have so many friends among the members of the *ton,* after all. Not among the ladies, of course, but among many of their husbands, as well as the bachelors. I believe that Harriette actually has her own box for the season, and one at the Royal Opera House, as well. A gift from some 'friend,' I have heard. Although I do not doubt she could easily afford the fee."

"Lady Brompton, how can you admit to knowing so much about her?" Trevor teased and was once more cracked across the knuckles by her fan.

"My boy, a female of my age is privileged to hear any number of things, although she does not speak of them before the children."

Holly started to ask another question, then decided not to do so. No one wished to tell her what she wanted to know. Even Felicia, although Felicia would doubtless explain matters to her when they arrived home. Felicia, aware of her sister's brief attention span, hoped the matter would be forgotten by that time. *She* had known there were such creatures, but how could one explain them to Holly?

Celia began pointing out other people to Holly—ones who were less reprehensible than the famous courtesan—but her grandmother poked her with her fan, ordering, "Hush. The play is beginning."

The girl obediently fell silent, but she was almost the only person in the theater to do so. Most of the audience continued its chattering, ignoring the appearance of the actors. After all, one came to the theater to see and be seen, perhaps to make assignations or display a new conquest, not to observe the play. In the pit, the less affluent members of the audience shouted at one another, throwing orange peels and nut shells from one seat to another, and frequently upon the stage, as well.

When Edmund Kean stepped before the footlights to make his first speech, however, there was a gradual hushing among the crowd. When John Kemble had been the darling of the London audiences, he had silenced his audience by the simple procedure of outshouting them.

Kean's method was different, although no one could explain how he could manage to quieten the gossiping that normally went on during a play. The only time he shouted was when the play called for him to do so. He was a small man with rather unprepossessing features, a man who would doubtless have been overlooked elsewhere, but he was master of the stage, able to convey all manner of emotions by his voice alone.

The first act was almost over when a murmur of voices rose throughout the theater, drowning out the actors' lines. Felicia looked questioningly at Lady Brompton, who merely nodded toward a central box, far more luxuriously furnished than the others, which had heretofore been unoccupied.

A number of people were entering the box, the pair in the center attracting the attention of the audience. The lady was of medium height, no longer young, and certainly not dressed to capture the curious glances that were being sent their way. It was the gentleman upon whom the crowd was gazing.

Like the lady, he appeared to be middle-aged. He was extremely stout, and made to appear even more so by the brilliance of his attire. The wide breast of his pink satin coat was nearly hidden by a number of jeweled orders, many of which he had designed from time to time when he could not find ones which pleased him.

As he stepped to the front of the box, the play ceased, the members of the cast bowing or curtsying toward the box. The gentleman pulled aside his coattails and seated himself, placing both hands over his large stomach and attempting to pull it in so that he would be less uncomfortable in his tight breeches, before graciously waving to the actors to proceed.

Celia pinched Holly to draw her attention. "That is the Prince Regent," she said, awestruck. "This is an event. We did not know he would be coming to the theater tonight. Grandmama and I saw him when we were invited to Carlton House last week."

Celia's excitement about having gone to Carlton House gave Holly something new about which to puzzle. There were hundreds, perhaps thousands, of houses in London. Why should this one be any different from the others? Were some people invited to go there while others were not? Oh, well, Felicia would explain it to her later, as well as telling her about the lady with the feathers. Felicia knew everything.

Perhaps she might even be able to tell her what this play was about. So many people seemed to be angry at one another, waving knives and swords about.

When the play was ended and the farce was given, she liked that better. Not that she understood much of it, either, but people around her were laughing, so it must have been amusing. She wished people would tell her why they were laughing, but when she tried to ask Celia, the other girl only giggled, said nothing. Holly thought that was rather unfair of her friend. She would like to have something to laugh about too.

She could not understand, either, why everyone should be so eager to see the Regent. He was merely a fat old man. Aside from his beautiful coat and all his jewels, he looked no different from Squire Tolbarth back home. And no one would have stopped a play and bowed to *him*.

She wished now they might have gone to a ball, after all, so that she might have danced with a handsome man or two, even if her feet did hurt. Still, Felicia appeared to have enjoyed the evening, and she did not think Felicia had much enjoyment from sitting about at balls while she danced. Felicia had always done so much for her, she knew. So, if Felicia was pleased with coming to the theater, what did it matter if she did not understand it?

When the farce was ended, everyone waited until the Regent had left before leaving their own seats. As they rose, Celia suggested, "Why do we not stop and have an ice before going home?"

Holly brightened at the idea, being fond of sweets, but Felicia said, "I think not. It is quite late, especially for us, who have not been long in town and accustomed to its ways. Perhaps another time."

"As you say, Aunt; Celia will forgive us for leaving so soon, I am certain, and her ladyship understands," Trevor told her, glancing at Lady Brompton, who has having great difficulty in keeping her eyes open. Her ladyship nodded agreement, and he sent a servant to have their carriages brought around. He was so agreeable at the moment that Felicia hoped this would be a good sign that she would hear no more from him about Mr. Harrison.

"I wish we might have had that ice," Holly said as they entered the house. However, she was yawning widely as she spoke, making Trevor laugh.

"If we had done so, you would have gone to sleep with your head in your plate," he teased. "And I do not think your hair would be improved by dipping it in the ice. If you do not sleep soon, you will be unable to gad about on the morrow."

"You are right," Felicia said. "Although it is the morrow already. You had best get to bed at once, Holly, and rest well."

"You, too, Auntie," he said. "You must look your best when your suitor comes to call."

He would have to spoil what had been a most pleasant evening by reminding her of James Harrison, Felicia thought as she glared at him, getting only his customary taunting smile in return. She noticed that Holly still lingered on the steps and transferred her glare to the girl.

"Why are you not going to bed?" Because of her anger at Trevor, she spoke more sharply than usual to Holly.

"There are some things about this evening that I do not understand," Holly protested. "a great number of them, in fact. I wish you would explain them to me."

Certainly, there would have been a great many things the girl had not understood; some of them puzzled Felicia. "I shall tell you everything in the morning," she promised. "Now you must get your rest."

However, she found herself unable to sleep for some time, while she marshalled arguments for tomorrow's meeting with James Harrison and strove to forget Trevor's comments that the young man's interest was only in her and not in Holly.

"I should be working upon my guest list for the ball," she muttered, but wondered if she should have the ball, after all. It had originally been her plan to announce Holly's betrothal on that occasion, preferably to James Harrison, but if he could not be persuaded to offer for Holly, to some other worthy gentleman. Yet, at the moment, Felicia was forced to own that she had made no progress in finding Holly a proper mate. Except for one gentleman, who seemed to have plans of his own.

Unwilling to face more of his remarks about the young gentleman, she delayed her descent to the breakfast room until she was certain Trevor must have left the house. As Mr. Harrison had requested to see her alone, she permitted Holly to omit the pianoforte practice she disliked and sent her, accompanied by her abigail, to call upon Celia Burley, requesting that Lady Brompton allow her granddaughter to spend the morning in shopping with Holly.

The old lady might think it strange that she should wish to send the girl out with Celia when they had spent some hours together just last evening, but as she herself was in the habit of behaving unexpectedly, she would not think it odd that Felicia might do the same.

Nor would she object to her granddaughter's going out, Felicia was certain, for had she not said she indulged Celia in almost everything she wished? Considering the forthcoming interview, she thought it would be better to have Holly out of the house for the present.

There was no way that she could expect Holly not to be a party to a visit from any of their friends, and it would be far easier for her to praise the girl to Mr. Harrison if she were not about. Too, he had owned he would be more at ease without her presence.

Evans could be relied on to curb any effort on Holly's part to indulge in paste buckles for her shoes, floss to trim her gowns, additional pairs of lace gloves or other such extravagances although, if Felicia had been present, she would have permitted the girl to purchase what she wished.

In an effort to convince Mr. Harrison that she was not the right choice for him, Felicia donned her soberest morning gown of gray with a high collar and tiny ruff. For the first time, she pinned a cap over her wig. "This should serve to convince him of my advanced age," she told herself, hoping she was right.

James Harrison seemed slightly surprised by the picture she presented, but his halt in the doorway was only for a moment. Then he hurried toward her, catching both her hands in his and raising them to his lips.

"You are alone, as I had hoped you would be." His tone was of one who had been granted a great boon.

"Yes." She seated herself, being careful not to choose the sofa, fearing he might take this as an invitation to sit beside her. She motioned him to a seat facing her, and said, "I thought it might be better not to have Holly present at this time. And, of course, although my nephew is a gentleman, he is not the head of the family, so you would not need to speak to him."

"No, no, I should prefer not to speak to Mr. Thomas. I somehow have the thought that he is laughing at me for my feelings."

"Oh, that is merely Trevor's way. I doubt if he is ever serious about anything. Most of you young gentlemen are like that, I have found. It was far different in my youth." Was she making the reference to the difference in their ages too strong? No, he appeared to take her at her word.

"I am not like that, my dear lady. Nothing could be more serious than my feelings for you."

Felicia wished that she were holding a fan, or anything that might occupy her hands. She found herself so nervous that it was difficult to refrain from twisting her fingers together. She should remain perfectly calm while she set about convincing him that Holly would suit him far better than she. She knew this, but found it impossible to control her feelings. "How remiss of me not to offer you tea," she said desperately, rising and reaching for the bell pull.

James was on his feet immediately, catching her hands and drawing her down to sit at his side. "No tea," he told her. "Only the opportunity to tell you how deeply I have come to care for you."

"It is kind of you to say that." She tried to free her hands, but he refused to release them, and she thought it too undignified to struggle. "A woman of my years must indeed be flattered by the respect of one so much younger than herself."

"Not respect, my dear Felicia. Oh, I know you have not

given me the right to call you that, but I have done so to myself since I first saw you, so I trust that you will forgive me for the familiarity. I do respect you, of course; that was not what I meant. But you must know of my adoration. And do not speak of years. The few between us are of no consequences."

Although she knew he was at least five years older than she, Felicia felt she must continue to play the middle-aged lady. If she emphasized the fact of age, she might have the best chance of turning his interest away from her.

"I have heard," she commented, "that it is the custom in London for some young gentlemen to pretend an interest in ladies older than themselves. But I thought these were usually poets and the ladies persons of great rank of whom they might dedicate their work."

"There is no pretense about my interest in you, my dear lady." His voice was hoarse with emotion, and he had tugged at his cravat until its knot was beneath one ear. Leaning closer to her, he said, "I beg of you, let me prove the depth of my love for you."

"I must beg your pardon, Aunt," Trevor Thomas said from the doorway. "Hastings neglected to tell me that we were entertaining visitors this morning. I trust that I do not intrude."

James started as if he had been stung, releasing Felicia's hands, and turning to glower at the newcomer. Why did that young Welsh fool have to come in just at this time? Why must he be forever underfoot? he thought angrily.

Aware that her face was crimson, Felicia said, "We were about to have some tea, Trevor. Will you ring for it, as you are already on your feet?"

"Certainly." He stepped toward the bell pull, but the other man rose hastily.

"I regret that I shall be unable to remain for tea. If you

will excuse me—" He dashed toward the door, almost colliding with Hastings.

"Mr. Harrison is leaving, Hastings," Trevor said. "Call his carriage. Then will you have tea served to my aunt and me?"

As the outer door closed behind Mr. Harrison, Felicia turned angrily to her "nephew" and demanded, "Do you know what you have just done? You *knew* he was planning to call this morning."

"Certainly. You told me as much. No, that is not quite true. You do not tell me your plans, do you? I overheard you agree to the meeting as I was fetching your drink yesterday. Or did you tell me later? I am not certain how I knew it, but I did, of course."

"Stop babbling! If you knew he was to be here, why did you interfere?"

"I thought I was rescuing you from a situation which threatened to become unpleasant. That is, I suppose that you did wish to be rescued, did you not?"

"Yes—no—how do I know? But you have doubtless frightened him away. He will never wish to enter the house again. Now, how can I get him to offer for Holly?"

"My dear girl, there is no way that you can persuade him to turn his interest from you to Holly. You may as well resign yourself to that fact. For some reason I cannot understand, the fellow is besotted by a lady some years his senior—or at least, he thinks so. Even your cap and that gown apparently did not frighten him away, so you must believe he was serious."

"He said the difference in our ages was not so great, and that it did not matter," Felicia protested. It was one thing for her to refer to her pretended middle age; quite another to have it mentioned by others. Even Trevor, who knew it was a hoax.

Especially Trevor.

"You mean that you would have preferred that I had not come to your rescue when I did? You must realize that you would have been in his arms in another instant. Was that what you wished?"

"Certainly not, but he would never have presumed so far—"

"There are times I think you are quite as birdwitted as Holly. I should have allowed him to maul you, gentleman though he claims to be."

"Oh, I am grateful—I suppose. Except that I do not know now what I am to do."

"Do not encourage him."

"I have done nothing of the kind," she said furiously, "except to try to interest him in Holly."

"Well, if you cannot see that will be useless, there is nothing more I can do for you." He stalked out of the room past Hastings, who was supervising the maidservant with the tea.

"Oh, take that away!" Felicia shouted and ran up the stairs to her room. Sober thought showed her that Trevor was doubtless right—she was not going to be able to interest James Harrison in Holly. She must begin her plans anew with some other gentleman in mind.

# * Eight *

FELICIA WAS STILL fulminating over Trevor's latest interference in her life when Holly dashed into the house, her bonnet askew, her reticule dangling by a single strand, while Evans hurried after her, crying, "Please, Miss, take care. A lady does not run about in the streets. People will think you a hoyden."

"Oh, Felicia," Holly managed between gasps for breath. "You can never guess what happened! Never in all this world!"

"What has happened?" her sister asked, greatly alarmed, because Holly was not given to outbursts of this sort. "Have you had an accident of some kind? Evans, please tell me—"

"Oh, my la—I mean Miss Arsdale—no, there was no accident, but the way the young miss has been capering about in the street, and before some of the members of the *ton* too."

"Oh, Holly, you did not behave so wildly, and after all the pains we have been taking to make everyone approve of us—"

"That is not important," Holly retorted in what her sister thought a callous manner, one which was totally unlike her. She customarily listened carefully to whatever Felicia told her she should do, and obeyed, as long as she could recall what had been said. "You do not understand, Felicia. It is the most wonderful thing. I could not believe it myself."

"Perhaps I could understand, if you explained matters to me," Felicia said, making an attempt to keep her patience, while she wondered what was affecting Holly in this way.

"That is what I am doing, if you will only listen to me. Celia and I were strolling along on Bond Street, looking into the shops with Evans and her abigail, when a man came dashing across the street, right under the noses of a team of dray horses, and calling my name. I thought he certainly must be run down, but he escaped. Felicia, it was Andrew Marsh! Imagine Andrew being in London!"

Felicia closed her eyes; she could imagine all too well what Andrew's presence in the city could mean to her plans. He would take one look at her and declare to all who would listen that she was not the middle-aged spinster she was pretending to be, and would demand to be told what sort of may-game she was playing.

Andrew would know, too, that Trevor Thomas was no relation of theirs, and it was impossible to believe that he would keep his discovery of Trevor's presence in the house to himself. He was far too straitlaced to dismiss such a matter.

In Felicia's mind, the circumstances of Trevor's being in the house were so involved that there would be no way of explaining them to Andrew's satisfaction. How could she do so, without telling him that it had resulted from her wish to take Holly away from his influence? Naturally, such an explanation would not please him, and he would blame Felicia for allowing Holly to be a part of what would appear to him as an ugly situation which, in a way, Felicia could only agree that it was.

Before nightfall, the *ton* would ring with the story that two young females—no one would call them ladies after they heard his tale—were residing under the same roof with a strange young man. Holly's chances for a good marriage would be ruined, and if he spread the story in Leamington, as he was certain to do, they would not even be able to go home again.

"What is he doing in London?" Her tone was sharper than usual, but Holly did not notice, being too engrossed in her own news.

"Oh, he has come on some kind of an errand for his uncle. He did not know where we were living; I am not certain he even knew we had come to London for I did not have an opportunity to tell him that we were coming here, although I had wanted to do so. But he saw me and ran across the street to greet me. Is it not wonderful to have someone here who knows us?"

I should have preferred a visitation of the black plague, Felicia thought. "How long will he be here? And is he coming to call on us?" If he did call, there was no way she could keep Trevor's presence a secret from him. Holly was certain to tell him about their "cousin"—and the man himself had the habit of showing up at the worst times.

"No." Holly drooped as she made the admission. "I asked him to come, truly, I did, Felicia. But he said that his uncle was expecting him to meet with some gentlemen this evening. Can you recall his uncle having any business in London? I cannot. I do not recall his ever saying anything about an uncle."

Felicia knew that if Andrew had spoken about any number of relatives, Holly would have listened to him in her customary intent manner, then would have forgot the matter within moments. However, she said nothing, unwilling to keep Andrew Marsh in her sister's thoughts longer than was necessary.

"And he must go home early tomorrow morning," Holly was complaining. "I think it shameful that we cannot have

even a short visit with him." She looked as if she might
burst into tears at any moment.

Felicia turned away for an instant so that her sister could
not see the sigh of relief she could not hide. Then she said,
"You must not begin weeping, Holly, you will ruin your
eyes if you do so. And you ought not to weep over
something as unimportant as this. Certainly, if Andrew
Marsh had wished to call upon us, he would have found
time to do so."

"But it is *not* unimportant. And how could he call if he
did not know where to find us? We did not give anyone in
Leamington our direction—"

For precisely this reason, Felicia told herself. Her sole
purpose in bringing Holly to London was to free her from
the sort of background in which she had been raised and to
give her the opportunity of a better future. She had not
wished for *anyone* from home to be able to find them. It was
purely unfortunate that Andrew Marsh had done so.

"He would have known where we are, you may be
certain, or he could have learned our direction if he wished
to know it." Felicia forced herself to speak carefully. Holly
must be convinced to give over this idea of wishing for
Andrew's visit, yet she should not be overset, which could
happen so easily. "You must realize, child, that a man like
Andrew Marsh must have many other interests than a pair of
sisters, merely because they once lived near him."

"But we have known each other for years, Felicia. We
were always such close friends." She had obeyed the order
not to weep, but still spoke mournfully and the corners of
her mouth drooped in a manner which dismayed Felicia.

More than friends, Felicia thought. It had been clear for
several years that Andrew was deeply smitten with Holly, as
was every other young man who had seen her. She did not
think that Holly had seriously returned his regard; she had
doubts that her sister was capable of feeling any deep

emotion. But if she had not intervened and taken Holly away, there was little doubt in Felicia's mind that Andrew would have won her. Holly was much too persuadable for her own good.

"It is true that he was once our friend, but you must understand, Holly, all of that was in the past."

"Not so long ago."

It was unlike Holly to argue, but Felicia went on, knowing she could soon bring her sister around to her way of thinking once more, "You were merely children, after all. Now that we have come to London, everything has changed. Andrew would not fit into our life here. Can you imagine him taking tea with the new friends we have made, or leading you out to waltz at Almack's?"

"N-no," Holly owned. "He would not like that. He calls such things foolishness."

"Certainly he would not want to do as we do. Doubtless he would even tell you that your pretty new gowns were unfit to wear for every day, as they would be at home."

Holly looked thoughtful at that; she had not expected that her old friend might not have liked her beautiful new clothes. Felicia was happy that she had thought of that argument. More than anything else, it might convince Holly to forget about Andrew.

"So it is best that he will not be here longer, for we could not take him among our new friends. It would not be the thing, for him or for them, and everyone would be made unhappy. Now, I wish you to rest for a time, then we shall decide which of your new gowns you shall wear tonight. You must be exceptionally pretty."

"Where are we going?" Even through her misery, Holly felt a surge of interest.

"I thought we might follow the example of some of our friends and visit several balls. We have received so many invitations that we can never get about to all of them unless we call at several homes in one evening. That is the way of most of the *ton*. It will be tiring, however, so you will need your rest." It would also keep Holly so occupied that she would forget completely about Andrew Marsh.

Holly nodded and obediently went up to her room. Felicia then gave her attention to Evans, who was still exhibiting signs of outrage at the younger girl's behavior. "And what about Miss Burley? Surely, you did not leave her alone on the street?"

"No, my—Miss. I would never be so remiss in my duties. Since the carriage was not immediately available, I wasted no time in waiting for it to arrive, but summoned a hackney and saw that she and her maid had entered it before I hurried after Miss Holly. But I must tell you, my—Miss, that this is not the sort of behavior to which my young ladies are accustomed."

"I am certain it is not," Felicia said soothingly. "But you must remember that Miss Holly is quite young and— impressionable."

"Yes, Miss, I must say that she is." Worse than that, she told herself. The girl is little better than a moonling. If the older one plans to bring one of the gentlemen of the *ton* up to scratch, she had best do so before they learn the truth.

Unaware of the poor opinion Evans had of her mistress, Felicia smiled at her and said, "So we must forgive her this little outbreak, but I hope there will be no chance of anything of that kind happening again." And there would not be if Andrew Marsh was truly leaving in the morning. She doubted if any of their other neighbors would come to London. Her masquerade would be safe, and soon, she hoped, she would have Holly married.

Evans's smile was sour, but she reflected that she was receiving a better wage here than she had done in her last position, or would doubtless be able to do so again, so said nothing more. It was clear to her that Miss Arsdale would brook no criticism of the girl, regardless of what sort of hoydenish acts she might have committed.

It was not, Evans told herself, as if she were a long-time servitor who would have been free to speak her mind and give good advice to her mistress. If she had not already jeopardized her position by what she had just said, she must not do anything that might do so now. Silence was the best thing, in the circumstances.

Despite Felicia's words, Holly was certain that she would never recover from the fact that she could not spend more time with Andrew, would have no opportunity to show him off to her friends, who would envy her for knowing one who was so handsome. He was even better looking than their cousin Trevor. "Well, almost," she qualified, for she doubted anyone could outshine Trevor.

Nonetheless, by the time she had napped briefly, she awoke eager for the evening's activities. Felicia had judged the younger girl aright. Her disappointment at not being able to invite Andrew Marsh to visit them was forgotten in the pleasure of wearing another new gown, this one of white silk, covered by gauze embroidered with tiny blue flowers. A small wreath of matching flowers held her coppery curls in place, and both her shoes and long gloves were of the same shade of blue.

Felicia thought her sister looked more than ever like a fairy-tale princess, and Trevor, waiting to escort the pair of them to the first of several balls they planned to attend tonight commented, "I wager you will break at least a dozen hearts tonight, Cousin."

"No more than you will," Holly told him with a trace of sauciness, unusual for her. It appeared that she might be learning something of the flirtatious manners of the other young ladies of the *ton*. Let her flirt a bit, her sister thought. But better with someone else than this man who might break her heart.

"Careful, Holly, you will cause his head to swell," Felicia warned her.

Holly peered closely at her "cousin." "Is it truly swelling?" she wanted to know.

"That is only a saying," Trevor told her with a laugh. "It means that if you praise me so much, you will cause me to think much too well of myself."

"And certainly you do not need help to do that, do you?" Felicia's tone was caustic. To herself, she owned that it was quite probable that he would break any number of hearts tonight—if there were any he had not already broken. But not Holly's, she begged. The girl would not long remember him if he went away, but even in a short time, she could be badly hurt.

In his long-tailed coat and evening pantaloons of deepest blue, his immaculate cravat worn in the style known as *Trone d'Amour* (although she did not recognize it as anything beyond the ordinary), his black hair gleaming as brightly as his evening shoes, there was no doubt that Trevor was a handsome man. Not that Felicia would have shown by the slightest glance that she was aware of the fact.

He had agreed at once to Felicia's suggestion that they attend as many balls as possible this evening. She was not surprised that he should do so; the more places they visited, the better his chances of finding the wealthy wife he sought.

Before much longer, there would be any number of eager young ladies hoping that he would throw the handkerchief in their direction. Felicia told herself that she could hardly wait for the day he announced that he was leaving them to be married.

Felicia herself was again wearing a gown of her favorite deep lavender color, this time trimmed with a tiny white ruching about the neck and at the cuffs. But again she told herself that she would remain unnoticed when she was accompanied by so handsome a pair as Holly and Trevor.

Or if she won any notice it would be because she was again bareheaded among a group of ladies in elaborate turbans topped with myriads of feathers.

Still, as he slipped a fur-trimmed wrap around her shoulders, Trevor said so softly that Holly could not have heard him. "I am happy that you have dispensed with the cap once more, Auntie. I much prefer you without it."

Startled, she turned to stare up at him, but he was seemingly intent upon guiding Holly to the carriage, and he said nothing more during the ride. Felicia was half convinced that she must have imagined the comment, although why she should imagine any such words from him, she could not have told. It was totally unlike Trevor to be so complimentary—toward her.

Tonight, she seated herself between Lady Brompton and a lady she had not met earlier, but who was introduced to her as Mrs. Conniston. The lady was extremely tall, her height more noticeable because of the two large plumes which rose heavenward from her turban. Between her and Lady Brompton, Felicia felt herself safe, at least at this first ball, from any attentions from James Harrison.

She knew she could not depend upon such protection at the next affair they attended, for Lady Brompton had declared that one ball in an evening was the best that she could manage, no matter how Celia might wish for more. However, she did not see the young gentleman amid the crush of their next ball. As was customary, several balls and routs were taking place each evening, everyone determined to invite as many of the *ton* as was possible during the brief Season.

James could not know which of them she would attend, and would hardly wish to make himself a laughingstock by trailing her from one to another. Without his presence, Felicia felt herself free to concentrate upon choosing a proper young man to replace him in her plans for Holly. She was eager to finish the plans for *her* ball, the one to announce Holly's engagement, but the right gentleman must be chosen first.

A number of gentlemen surrounded her sister, as was usual, but she discarded them, one by one. Two or three, she had learned, were hardened gamesters, doubtless seeking wives with sufficient dowries to permit them to continue their deep play. It would be simple to discourage them by allowing them to know that Holly's portion would be quite small.

On the other hand, Mr. Taylor did not appear to be interested in gaming, and was certainly wealthy enough to fill her requirements, but she had heard that he was addicted to such sports as fox-hunting. She knew that Holly would never to happy with such a gentleman. She would doubtless swoon the first time she heard the tale of his running down a fox.

Sir Geoffrey Maubin was mild-mannered, almost too much so, for Holly needed someone who would make decisions for her. However, he would expect the lady of his choice to listen to reams of his poetry, which Felicia thought florid but without substance. Not only to listen, but to discuss it with some show of intelligence.

Holly, who had never opened a book except when Felicia had ordered her to study, or memorized a line of verse, would be lost in any such discussion. Her wide-eyed appearance of interest might deceive him during a dance, but could not be depended upon to do so during an entire courtship. Felicia feared she must rule out Sir Geoffrey, as well as Mr. Taylor.

By the time the weary trio made their way home in the early dawn, Felicia was forced to own to herself that she had not found anyone nearly as suitable for Holly as James Harrison would be—if only he had not formed this foolish attraction to her rather than to her sister. Still, there were several weeks remaining in the Season, so she should be able to choose a substitute suitor and persuade Holly that he was the ideal man for her.

She had settled upon a date in the last week of the Season, and had made up her guest list. The next step was to have her invitations made up. She would not mention the reason for the event on the invitations, so there was still time to find the proper husband. She had no doubt that, even without the hint of a betrothal, her ball would draw a crowd. Everyone would be wondering what the eccentric Felicia Arsdale had in mind this time.

Once Holly was safely married, she could tell Trevor to do his worst, if he dared. A gentleman of the *ton* would not take it lightly if another were to cast slurs upon his bride and, while she doubted that James—or whomever she chose—would challenge Trevor, there was doubtless something that could be done to silence him.

For herself, she would either go home or seek some suitable employment, if it was necessary for her to do so. It would be best if she left London, so that no one in the family would be shamed by having a relative working as a hired companion nearby.

It was almost eleven o'clock when Felicia arose and dressed. "This gadabout life is making me quite lazy," she reproached herself, forgetting that she had not retired until nearly the hour of five.

Such habits might do for members of the *ton*, but she would have to take care not to become accustomed to them, for she would have to fend for herself once Holly had been safely married. And employers, if she were fortunate enough to find one, expected those who served them to be about early in the day.

She had scarcely had time to swallow a cup of tea and nibble a bit of bread and butter before callers swarmed into the house. Mrs. Headly was again among the foremost, eager to relay the terrible news, since the victim was again a person of some importance.

During the early hours of the morning, the thief—from his actions, he was surely the same one as before, everyone said—had entered Lady Foresham's bedchamber and made off with her sapphires, the last gift of her late husband. A gift, rumor had it, that had been meant for his mistress, but when they were mistakenly delivered to her ladyship, he had no choice but to pretend that she had been the intended recipient.

"But that is not the worst," Mrs. Headly confided with ghoulish pleasure, meaning the theft, not the rumor, which she had thoroughly enjoyed repeating at an earlier time to all who would listen, and had, in fact, been the one who was responsible for beginning it. "It seems that Lady Foresham is a light sleeper and heard him moving about. But he must have heard her, as well. Before she could scream for assistance, the scoundrel seized her and fastened a gag over her mouth, then bound her hands to the bedpost, so that she could not reach the bell pull. A housemaid discovered her, but, he was long gone by that time."

"Could the lady describe him?" Felicia asked, struck by a sudden suspicion.

A number of voices gave conflicting answers. The window curtains were closed so that it was too dark for her to see him; the man was masked; Lady Foresham's eyesight was poor; she was too hysterical to give a good description; of course she would know him if she saw him again, but she knew she would die if she must face those evil eyes, eyes that gleamed like fire, another time.

Felicia's head was spinning by the time her callers had gone in search of another listener who had not already heard their tale. Despite a great number of conflicting accounts, one thing was certain—the thief could not be described by his latest victim, even though she had been aroused by his presence in her bedchamber.

Felicia was certain, however, that *she* could describe the man. She had not heard Trevor leave the house after they returned home last night, but it did not matter. What mattered was that Lady Foresham's was one of the balls they had attended last evening. As for his going out, had he not been able to slip *into* this house in broad daylight, with all the servants about? If he could do that, he should have no trouble in leaving just as quietly, or in entering the room he planned to rob.

It could not be coincidence that each of the thefts had taken place immediately after she had taken Trevor Thomas, as her nephew, to visit the victim. He had been given an opportunity to look over the place, and more importantly, to see what jewels he might take. And had he not praised the skill of the thief?

"How could I have been so foolish as not to have seen at once what he had in mind?" she asked herself.

At that moment, Trevor descended from the upper floor, looking, if such a thing was possible, more handsome than ever. A life of crime must agree with him, Felicia told herself.

"Have all the gabblers gone?" he asked. "I was about to come down for my breakfast when I heard them and thought it best to stay where I was till they had left. They would have taken away my appetite."

"I do not think there was any need for you to be concerned," Felicia said, her tone dripping acid. "After all, it seems you were not recognized by your latest victim."

"What do you mean by that?"

"As if you did not know. Lady Foresham says that the thief was masked."

"He was? What thief was that?"

The bewilderment he displayed was almost enough to

convince her. However, she knew only too well how he could feign innocence. "It was bad enough," she said angrily, "when I thought you only wished me to introduce you to the *ton* so that you could find a rich wife. I could overlook that because I know now that many so-called gentlemen do the same. But you are something far worse than a fortune hunter—you want to meet wealthy women so that you can steal their jewels."

There was a malicious glint in the blue eyes as she completed her tirade. "But have you thought, my dear Auntie, if a gentleman wishes to win a wealthy wife, he must have some money of his own to offer? And what better way to obtain it than to take it from those who have more than they need?"

"So it is true!"

"If you could prove me to be the jewel thief, which you cannot,"—there was a longer any hint of amusement in his tone—"you still could say nothing. *You* have been my sponsor, so would be found as guilty as I. Think what it would do to Holly's future to have you branded as my accomplice, then decide if you wish to attempt unmasking me."

"I believe it would be worth the risk to rid myself of your presence." she retorted. "I could say that I had been taken in by you, as everyone else has been."

"Ah, yes, my dear—but you forget—if you talk, so shall I. And *I* can prove the accusations I shall make. You cannot."

Before she could think of a proper retort, he said, "I think, under the circumstances, I shall seek my breakfast elsewhere," and walked out of the house, passing James Harrison on the steps.

That young gentleman looked after the other until he had passed out of sight around the corner. He wished no further interruptions to his courtship of the lady he had chosen.

Beneath her breath, Felicia was making the comments she would have liked to make to Trevor when Hastings appeared at the breakfast room door to inform her that Mr. Harrison had called.

In her present mood, she could have wished the young gentleman in China, but there was nothing she could do but to tell Hastings to show him into the drawing room. "I shall be with him in a moment," she said, pausing only to force herself to smile before she followed the servant into the room.

Presenting her with a bouquet so large that she must hold it in both hands, James started his rehearsed speech, then paused, aware that Hastings was still standing near the door, waiting for his mistress to hand him the flowers. When she had done so and the servant had departed, closing the door after him, Felicia said quickly, "It was good of you to call today. I suppose that you, like everyone, have been discussing the theft at Lady Foresham's home last night."

"Well, no—I—" He was disconcerted by this talk of a theft when he had something far different on his mind, and spent several minutes attempting to find the best way to return to his subject.

As Trevor had made clear to her, she could not afford to denounce him as the thief, but there could be no harm in repeating what all London must be saying today, "The earlier thefts were bad enough, but when one thinks of that man daring to gag his victim and tie her to the bedposts . . . What sort of man would go to such lengths?" It was a relief to be able to say that much.

The young man opened his mouth, but Felicia rushed ahead, hoping to distract him from what she felt must be the true purpose of his call, "They say that her ladyship has been overcome by the vapors, and who can blame her? Not everyone is as brave as Lady Brompton, who says that *she* would have thrown her candlestick at the thief. But then,

she did not see him, so one cannot be certain if she would
have truly dared to threaten him—"

"My—Miss Arsdale," the young man's tone was one of
desperation, "I have *not* come to discuss Lady Foresham's
theft, or Lady Brompton's for that matter. There are other
things that are much more important."

"Of course, you wish to see Holly. However, I fear that
she is quite a slugabed today, as were we all. We have not
accustomed ourselves to so many late nights, being new to
the city."

"Nor did I wish to meet with Miss Holly, as I have told
you before." His voice was stronger now. At least, they
were discussing his purpose in being here, rather than the
misfortunes of others. "Nor have I any wish to see your
nephew, whom I passed on my way into the house, I am
happy to say. I feel that he does not approve of me, although
I have never given him any cause. Or perhaps he feels that
I should obtain his permission first; does he consider
himself the head of the family?"

*"Trevor?"* She hoped her laugh was convincing; merely
thinking of Trevor was again enough to arouse her anger.
"Certainly not. Or if he does, he ought not to do so. He only
joined us since we came to London; we were unacquainted
with him before that time."

He drew a breath of relief. "Then you do not mind that I
speak directly to you?"

Since there appeared to be no way to prevent him from
speaking, Felicia said, "Certainly, you may say whatever
you wish to me."

"I am certain that you must be aware of my great
admiration for you, so great that I fear I may have been
overbold on my last visit. If so, I must beg you to forgive
me."

"N-no, I was not offended." This was true, but who
could have told, however, how far his ardor might have

carried him if Trevor had not come into the room at that moment? And Trevor was not here to interrupt them on this occasion.

"As I said, you must be aware of my feelings. I know you have attempted to discourage my suit because of the difference—which truly is slight—in our ages. But I assure you, it means nothing to me. M-Miss Arsdale,"—he dropped to his knees, unfortunately reminding Felicia of his impromptu kneeling before her in the carriage—"will you do me the honor of becoming my wife?"

Felicia bit her lip, both to choke down her laughter at the memory, knowing his feelings would be injured if he thought she remembered that unfortunate occasion, and wondering how best to answer him. She had no desire to accept his offer; his position meant nothing to her, except, she owned silently, as a husband for Holly. However, he had made it plain that it was not Holly he wanted, but herself. Trevor's mocking warnings came into her mind.

Still, should she consent to his suit, her own position in the *ton* would be assured and there would be no problem in finding the right sort of husband for her sister. She did not love James, of course, but did that matter so greatly? It was not the habit, she understood, for members of the *ton* to expect to find love in marriage. When she was quite a young girl, she had sometimes dreamed of romance, but when it became necessary for her to care for Holly, she had put aside such thoughts.

Despite the fact that James was at least five years older than she, instead of being younger, as he thought, he seemed almost childish compared to . . . to . . . To Trevor, she was forced to tell herself, then hated herself for the thought.

She thought suddenly that, if she agreed to marry James, she could still hold her ball to announce the event. And she would see that Trevor was the one who should make the announcement. She would enjoy that, knowing he would have to accept the fact that he would no longer be able to taunt her with his threats. Nor would he have a home here while he went about his thefts of jewels.

If she accepted James's offer, it would be necessary for her to explain the reason for her masquerade, but she thought that she would be able to make him understand her reasons. Perhaps it would be the wisest thing to give him her answer at once and save her explanations for a later date. Still . . .

"I must own, Mr. Harrison—"

"James."

"James, that I was not expecting your offer. I am honored, of course, that you should choose me. Will you allow me some time to think of it?"

"How long? I do not wish to press you, but—"

"Two or three days, at least, I should think. Such a serious matter should require at least that much time for consideration."

"I hope it will be no longer than that. But take whatever time you need. I can only hope your answer will be the one I wish."

"For that, you must wait, I fear." She did not know why she should delay if it was going to be necessary for her to accept him. But she felt she needed the time.

# * Nine *

A MAD GALLOP across the hills, Felicia said to herself as she adjusted the small beaver hat that matched her black riding habit and pulled on her York tan gloves, would have done much to relieve her feelings on this occasion. The hills, however, were far way, and a lady did not gallop her horse during rides in the Park, so she must make the best of matters.

Holly was not eager to ride, but her own riding habit of pale blue cloth with military trim, as well as the plume in her tiny hat, did much to overcome her aversion to the exercise. Since she was an indifferent horsewoman, Felicia thought it best that they ride early in the day when the Park was not crowded.

In the afternoon, they would change their gowns and order out the carriage to join the other members of the *ton*, who made their appearances to see and be seen. If they were fortunate, Felicia told herself, their "cousin" would have other plans and would not accompany them. She could imagine the disappointment his absence would make to the eager mamas and daughters they would meet, but even they could not expect that he would make an appearance every time Holly and Felicia did.

Being unsure of her mount, although Felicia had chosen

the most gentle the stable could provide, Holly was inclined to become somewhat nervous in crowds, and would have preferred to ride—if Felicia insisted upon their going out—when they were entirely alone. No matter how early they appeared, however, there were always others who also chose to ride in the early morning, and it seemed that there were a number of those who knew when and where she and Holly planned to ride. Felicia did not doubt that some of them bribed the stable hands to send word of their intentions.

However they managed to obtain the information, there would be a great many young gentlemen, idling along the paths to greet them and beg to be allowed to ride beside Holly. She never refused the attentions of any of them, and appeared to give each of them all her attention in return, but her sister knew that she understood little of the sporting talk that went on about them.

Felicia hoped that there would be one among the crowd who surrounded them whenever they rode who would make an acceptable offer for Holly. She knew that several young gentlemen had approached Trevor, thinking that, as the only male member of the family, he would be the one to grant their suits.

Although he had never told her he had done so, Felicia suspected, from the gentlemen's later behavior, that Trevor must have discouraged several of the applicants who were completely impossible—gazetted fortune hunters and the like. He would know such as they would be wasting their time if they hoped to win Holly Arsdale. Holly had no fortune to bring them.

Much as she might resent his interference in their lives, Felicia said nothing about his taking over some part of her duties in this case. She was only too happy to be relieved of the necessity of turning away the undesirables. However, he had informed most of them that Felicia was her "niece's" guardian, and must be the one to decide Holly's future.

Unfortunately, none of those who had spoken to her had been considered suitable, which caused her to wonder how much worse the ones had been whom Trevor had turned away. She was surprised at the number of young gentlemen of the *ton* who seemed to care more for the fit of their coats or the welfare of their horseflesh than of the preferences of the young ladies they met.

Each of them appeared so certain of his own importance that, beyond the surface politeness, they were all quite shallow creatures. To herself, she owned that she still held to the hope that James Harrison would change his mind and choose Holly instead of herself. That would have been so perfect a match, for James, at least, had thoughts about others than himself, and would doubtless be considerate of the female he married.

Disappointingly, Holly had not shown a preference for any of the gentlemen whose acquaintance they had made. She frequently compared one or another of them to her "cousin" Trevor, much to the other's disadvantage. This one was not so tall, that one's shoulders—with a blush for having noticed a gentleman's form—were narrower, a third did not dance nearly as well.

Accurate as the girl's observations about these admirers and about her "cousin" might be, Felicia had discouraged any signs of true interest on Holly's part for Trevor. "You know that he is only in London to find himself an heiress," she had said many times, certain that Holly would be badly hurt should she form a *tendre* for one who was nought but a blackguard.

Not even to Holly could she reveal that she was certain the man was using the protection of their "relationship" to give him the opportunity to steal from their newfound acquaintances, so she merely said, "That is his only reason for coming to London."

"Yes, I know," Holly replied, "and you have told me that we are not heiresses, so he would not be interested in either of us." The thought that she might be passed over for a wealthier young female did not appear to cause Holly any unhappiness. If Holly ever had a thought, her sister said to herself.

"It is only that he is quite the handsomest of all the gentlemen of the *ton*," Holly went on. "I do not see why he should not find the right wife."

Felicia was happy that Holly's interest in Trevor went no deeper than her admiration for the other's appearance. It might be necessary for her to keep her silence about Trevor's thefts; painful as it was for her to do so, she did not doubt that he would ruin Holly's chances if she betrayed him.

Still, she *would not* permit Holly to fall in love with a thief, even if it meant that she must give up her plans for her and return home. It would be better to allow Holly to make her choice among their country neighbors than to form a *tendre* for such a scoundrel.

She might be unable to have Trevor brought to justice for his crimes, but Felicia knew that if she agreed to marry James Harrison, the young Welshman could be sent on his way. She need no longer fear what he might do or say. The Earl of Cranston was a power in England and, although James was the younger son, his wife would be protected from the slurs that Trevor threatened. When she could hold that threat over his head, Trevor would be forced to give up his thievery and leave London.

She knew that James would be only too happy to see the last of Trevor; for some reason she could not understand, the two had never become friends. Neither of them had been so ungentlemanly as to air their disagreements in public, but it seemed to her that, whenever they met, the air bristled with their mutual dislike.

Felicia was reminded of a pair of mastiffs facing one another—no, rather a mastiff and a terrier—each ready, on a signal, to go for the other's throat. The two men were so different; James was completely a gentleman, and she knew that Trevor's good manners were no more than a veneer to hide his inner baseness.

"I confess I can see no way out," she said half-aloud as she and Holly turned their mounts homeward from Hyde Park.

"What are you talking about, no way out of what, Felicia?" Holly wanted to know.

"Oh, just a small problem, one that that need not concern you." She could see no reason to explain anything to Holly about her quandary; there was nothing she could do to help, and Felicia would not permit her to worry herself about it.

"Whatever it is, I am certain you will know what to do," her sister said with a smile. Felicia sometimes worried about things, Holly knew. Whatever they might be, she always told Holly not to bother herself about them. And Felicia always knew what she was about, Holly was certain of that. She would solve whatever it was that worried her.

"Yes, I know what I must do." She must explain to James, of course, that she did not love him, but since the members of the *ton* seldom married for love, she did not think he would consider that a bar to their happiness. Could she manage to spend the rest of her life with a man who interested her so little? For Holly's sake, she was certain she could do so.

She knew that certain ladies of the *ton* found interests outside of their marriage, but she did not think she would be able to do so—at least, not in the form of some other gentleman. If she gave her word to James, she would keep it.

The ride had done nothing to clear her mind—she was not certain that a gallop would have done so—but she returned to Grosvenor Square determined that she would delay no longer, but would send a message to James today, asking him to call upon her.

He would know her reason at once, so there would merely be the matter of explaining to him about her masquerade. Certainly, he would understand that she had felt there was no other way for her to bring Holly to London, and why she had thought it important to settle her sister's future.

She suspected that, rather than wishing to have Holly live with them, James would do his utmost to find her a proper husband. He would know that, as long as she was unmarried, Felicia would feel herself responsible for her sister, and would put Holly's concerns above all else, even the concerns of a husband. Unquestionably, among his many friends, there would be a gentleman who was exactly right for Holly.

Having steeled herself to accept the inevitable, it was rather oversetting to find a message waiting for her from Lady Brompton.

Celia, the old lady had written, had expressed a wish to attend Vauxhall that evening, but her grandmother felt that such an excursion, which would include a great deal of walking, was beyond her strength. She begged that Felicia would take her place as chaperon to Celia, and, of course, to Holly, who would doubtless find the gardens as exciting as Celia expected to do. No doubt, she added, the young gentleman could be persuaded to lend them his escort for the evening, as he was in the habit of doing.

"I should not consent, of course, to Celia's going there upon the nights when a masquerade is held," Lady Brompton's message continued. "For who knows what rogues might lurk behind those masks? There is no way of ensuring that none but members of our class attend these affairs. I should suppose the mere fact that they could be masked would enable some of the worst, both men and women, to ply their customary trades. And doubtless, even some gentlemen would take advantage of the fact that they were masked to behave most improperly. Tonight, I understand that there will be merely music and the customary fire-works. The children should enjoy the latter, if not the former."

Felicia smiled to herself. Again, Lady Brompton had decided upon short notice to grant one of the girl's wishes, and, as before, was expecting her new friend to come to her assistance. Of course, they must go; she had no doubt that Holly would truly enjoy such an outing as much as Celia would do.

For several moments, Felicia considered sending a message to James Harrison, asking if he would be kind enough to escort them to the gardens. That idea was quickly discarded; James would doubtless accept this request as a favorable answer to his suit. Without stopping to remember that she had come home from her ride determined to give him exactly such an answer, she was unaccountably happy to have a reason for delaying her reply.

She might have asked him to call for her answer earlier in the day, but she told herself that a visit to Vauxhall was scarcely the proper way to celebrate a betrothal. She could speak to him later, if she could not find some other solution to her problem.

Since they could scarcely make such an outing without an escort, Felicia's refusal to send word to James left her with no alternative but to request that Trevor accompany them, for there was no other gentlemen whose acquaintance was close enough for her to make such a request upon no more than a moment's notice.

She was reluctant to approach him, after the manner in which she had thrown accusations at him and his audacious answer. However, when she explained her reason for wishing to replace the ball which they had planned to attend with this diversion, he expressed his willingness to accompany them, so Lady Brompton was sent word that they would be happy to have Celia as a part of their group.

"Have you ever visited Vauxhall?" Celia asked as Trevor handed her into their carriage. All three answered in the negative.

"Nor have I, but I have heard so much about the gardens. I wish we might attend a masquerade there. It would be so exciting. But Grandmama does not approve of masquerades."

"I must agree with your grandmama that it would not be the thing, especially in a place like Vauxhall." Felicia knew she must sound exactly like the maiden aunt she appeared to be, but one must impress upon the young ladies the sort of danger they could face in such a place. She knew little about Vauxhall, but any sort of garden at night offered perils which had best be avoided. "Doubtless, there are a great number of unprincipled characters who might come to the gardens at that time, since the price of admission is not too great to exclude them."

She did not add that they were accompanied by one as devoid of principles as any they might encounter. At least, she had no fear that he would steal from either of them; neither carried anything of value, and he would not risk such a theft when he would be known to be guilty.

"My aunt is correct about the unsuitability of your attending a masquerade," Trevor added. "Many such people would consider the price of a ticket a paltry investment when compared with what they might garner during such an evening. Aided by the protection of a mask and domino, a rascally fellow could dip his fingers into a gentleman's pockets or a lady's reticule without much danger of being apprehended. Even worse, he might snatch the young lady herself and drag her into the Dark Walk."

"The Dark Walk?" Celia's voice held the mixture of dread and excitement the term might convey to one both innocent and eager.

"Yes, it is a place for young ladies to beware of. But I shall see that no one has a chance to entice you there."

"Stop teasing her, Trevor," Felicia ordered. She did not know Celia well enough to be certain such talk would not lead to nightmares. This would be poor repayment for Lady Brompton's kindnesses to them.

"Ah, but I am quite serious, Aunt. Danger lurks there for the unwary."

"Pay him no mind, Celia," Felicia advised. "Trevor only wishes to tease you."

"Crushed again," the young man said in despondent tones. "How can I play the hero if I do not convince the lady of her danger?" Still, he seemed to take the warning to heart, for he said no more about the dangers of the Dark Walk. He was well aware that Felicia would permit neither of the younger girls to come near the place.

The prosaic approach to the gardens was by driving across the bridge, but Trevor had managed to obtain a boat and had them rowed across the river, as was done when Vauxhall was new. This method of conveyance had held the fancy of many people since that time, so a number of boatmen still plied their trade.

As he had foreseen, Holly and Celia were thrilled by this conveyance, although both were a bit uneasy about its safety, neither having been aboard a boat before, and the pull of the tide being strongly felt in the small craft.

Trevor assured them that the boatmen had made hundreds

of trips across the river with no trouble, and that he had been careful to choose the safest of them. He had also obtained a box for them, so that they might sample the famous Vauxhall ham and other delicacies while listening to Mr. Hook's performance upon the organ and watching the other visitors strolling about.

They also took their turn at walking about to see the illuminated fantasies at the end of several of the walks, then returned to their box for some of the sweetmeats the girls enjoyed. There was dancing in the rotunda, but Felicia felt that this would be a different matter than appearing at a ball, and refused the pleas of both young ladies to be allowed to dance with Trevor.

"Aunt says 'no,'" he told them. "And, as usual she is in the right. You would appear somewhat fast if you were to be seen dancing here." He did not know whether or not this was true, for there were many among tonight's dancers who appeared to be ladies, but it was an argument they could not counter.

When the bell rang to signal the viewing of the Cascade, Trevor offered his arm to Felicia and shooed the younger ladies ahead of them to a point where the waterfall might be seen to best advantage. Feeling more in harmony with him than at any time in their acquaintance, Felicia said, "What a deal of trouble you are taking just to make them happy. You appear to know a great deal about this place."

"Nothing that I could not have learned by asking some questions. And I hope that it makes you happy, as well as the infantry."

"Well, yes, it does. I am happy that we came." For the evening, she had put aside the problem of Holly's future and was enjoying the present.

"Then my work has been well paid." He left her for an instant to discourage the pretensions of two young fops who had approached Celia and Holly. When they had been driven off, he suggested that the party return as soon as the Cascade performance was over, to listen to the singing of Mrs. Bland—although he personally had no desire to listen to a singer—until it was time for the displays of fireworks which were an important part of every Vauxhall evening. Then they would return home either by land or water, as the girls decided.

Felicia smilingly agreed to his suggestions, but wondered privately why he should put himself to so much trouble on their behalf. If he were seeking a wealthy wife, he must know that he had no chance with Celia; as much as she was attracted by him, Lady Brompton would put paid to any alliance between them—and he already had her grand-mother's diamonds, so could be seeking no more profit there.

After the excitement of the Vauxhall evening, Holly was extremely reluctant to take a morning ride. However Felicia insisted that they go, feeling that it was most important for Holly to meet as many gentlemen as possible. Who knows, she said silently, one of them might be so taken with her that he would offer at once. Then I should not have to consider marrying James.

It was a vain hope, of course. The crowd of admirers about Holly was as great as before, but no one appeared eager to go beyond the usual pleasantries, no one begged permission to call. There was no longer any reason for her to delay in giving James his answer.

When the footman opened the door for them, Hastings met them with a note for Holly. Celia was requesting her company upon a shopping trip. "You do not mind if I go with her, do you, Felicia?" Holly asked, passing her the note.

Although she had planned to have Holly spend some time again today at the pianoforte, Felicia knew her efforts in that

direction were wasted, as Holly would never become
proficient on the instrument.

Few of the young ladies who performed for their friends
and acquaintances could boast of any true expertise, but
Holly's efforts were worse than most. She appeared to have
no interest in the music, making her sister wonder if perhaps
she might be tone-deaf. At least she could not tell when she
struck discords which grated upon Felicia's ears.

Too, she thought it might be as well to have the girl
absent from the house for a time. When she returned, James
would doubtless have come and gone, and she could tell
Holly then of her decision to marry the young man.

Although it was a mere ten hours since they had Celia's
company at Vauxhall, Felicia said, "Certainly you may go;
you know I am always happy when you and Celia are
together. Hastings can order the carriage for you."

"No, Celia says that if I send her a message, she will
come for me. Her maid will go with us. Do you think it is
necessary for Evans to accompany us as well?"

Felicia had seen the servant Lady Brompton had assigned
to accompany her granddaughter, and had no doubt of the
woman's ability to curb the spirits of two young ladies,
should the necessity arise. There would be no running in the
street today.

"If you do not think that Celia will object to sharing her
maid with you, I think her company should be sufficient."

Holly ran upstairs to change her gown, leaving Felicia to
compose a message to Celia, accepting her invitation.
When she had done that, Felicia wrote her own message to
James and asked Hastings to have it sent after Holly had left
with Celia.

Changing into her prettiest gown, and wishing that she
had purchased something more youthful—although she had
not visualized there would be a need for anything of the
kind—Felicia debated for some time about whether or not

she should leave off the gray wig. However, she decided at last not to do so. There would be time enough to make so drastic a change in her appearance after she had spoken to James.

She heard the front door close and Hastings's voice as she made her way to the stairs. The butler came to the foot of the stairs as she descended, saying, "Mr. Harrison has arrived, my—Miss."

"Thank you." Was he never to lose the habit of nearly calling her "my lady"? Perhaps when he learned that she would be marrying James Harrison, he would make an effort to change the way he addressed her. "Has Mr. Thomas returned home?"

"No, m-Miss. I understand that he intends to be away for the entire day."

"Ah, good." At least, she would be spared his usual interference in her plans. "Thank you, Hastings, that will be all."

Feeling very much as she imagined a convicted felon must feel en route to the gibbet, rather than a young woman about to accept a proposal of marriage, Felicia entered the drawing room. She forced a smile, thinking a scream would better suit the occasion, as she said, "Good morning, James. I am happy that you received my message."

"Yes, although I was planning to call upon you today in any case."

There was something strange in his manner, something she could not understand. She thought she detected a difference in his tone, almost a coldness. Perhaps it is nothing more than the customary nervousness of a man when he knows it is too late to change his mind, she told herself.

In an attempt to put him at ease, she said, "It was good of you to come so quickly."

Instead of the eager reply she expected, his voice was

stiff when he replied, "As I said, I was preparing to come here when I received your message. I thought it best if we were to settle this matter as quickly as possible."

"Y-yes, of course." This scarcely sounded as if he were expecting her acceptance. Perhaps he had come to think that she was too old for him, after all. She hoped he had done so; it would not be too late for him to change his interest to Holly.

"It may speed matters if I tell you I have just come from having a talk with your—your nephew, I believe you call him. The second we have had of late."

"Trevor?" Had he said something more to disconcert the young gentleman? "You must know by now that his idea of humor is not quite the same as ours."

"That may be, but *was* he jesting when he told me that rather then being your nephew, he is someone you met only after you arrived in London, and he has been living here and allowing you to present him to the *ton* as a member of your family, when he is nothing of the kind?"

"He told you *that*?"

"He did, indeed. And more. And, as much as I should have preferred to disbelieve him, I remember discovering you in his arms at Lady Carelton's breakfast."

"In his—oh, you mean when I nearly fell and he saved me."

"I can see where you might prefer to have that tale believed, but it will not wash. There have been other incidents, as well, such as his interrupting us whenever we were alone together, although I was too blind to see them for myself."

"I do not know what you are talking about."

"I think you do. I wonder that you dare to bring a child like Holly into such a situation. But I suppose that you plan to marry her off in a hurry—was that why you attempted to attract my interest to her, I wonder—so that you may be free to conduct your liaison undisturbed?"

"My . . . ? *How dare you say such a thing?*" Her voice had risen to a shriek.

"Doubtless you have another name for it. Although I cannot think of a better one."

"There is nothing of what you appear to think—"

"I may as well tell you that I had met Mr. Thomas while on my way home after my last visit, and told him that I expected to have a favorable answer from you. And he laughed at me for having made you an offer, then told me what the situation truly was. He repeated the tale this morning when I met him. I am happy that I learned the truth before I saw you today. You can understand, of course, why I have withdrawn my offer of marriage."

He strode out of the room and out of the house before Felicia could think of a suitable retort. It was as well that he was beyond hearing when her voice returned, for she spared no words in her contempt for him.

"No," she said after a moment. "He is not to blame, of course, for thinking badly of me. I *have* deceived him, that is true, but certainly not in the way he thinks. It is Trevor who is responsible for all of this."

*How dared he?* After blackmailing her into agreeing to keep his secret by saying he would keep hers, the scoundrel had broken his word and told James everything—or almost everything. Apparently, he had also twisted matters to make her appear in the worst possible light.

She had been reluctant to accept James Harrison's offer, but to have it withdrawn was an insult. No more insulting, however, then the reasons he had given for doing so.

James had accused her of being Trevor's mistress, and he would not have done so without Trevor's telling him that. And who knew what else he might have said? And the impertinence of James, reading something evil into seeing her near the fountain when Trevor was holding her.

"But with what Trevor must have told him," she muttered, "I can see why he might leap to the wrong conclusion about that. That scoundrel *knew* why I was seeing James and deliberately said what he did about us."

Why, she asked herself, should she have expected honor from one she had always known to be an imposter and a blackmailer, whom she now knew to be a thief, as well? Doubtless, the reptile had even had the audacity to conceal his ill-gotten plunder in *her* house. What place could be safer? It would be close to his hand, and no one would think to search for it here; not even the eccentric Miss Arsdale would be expected to give shelter to a thief.

Well, she would find his hiding place. And then she would turn him and his loot over to the authorities. By saying what he had done to James, Trevor had put paid to her plans to find a respectable husband for Holly; *she* would put paid to his schemes to steal from her friends.

For all she cared, he could end his career upon the gibbet; it was no more than he deserved. In fact, she was sorry that it was no longer the custom to draw and quarter a criminal. She would have enjoyed thinking of his suffering.

She flung open the door to Trevor's room and gazed about. The room was neatly kept; to her eyes, suspiciously so. "Of course," she muttered, "I should not expect him to leave such things lying about. Perhaps even his servant does not know of his actions."

She dragged out piles of neatly starched cravats, silk stockings, items of male apparel that she ought not to know about, flinging everything upon the bed, making no attempt to keep her search a secret. He would know soon enough that his room had been ransacked when he discovered that the jewels were missing, so he might as well know it as soon as he came in. The sight of a small jewelry box elated her for a moment, but to her disappointment, it yielded nothing except several inconspicuous fobs and a pin with a flawed diamond.

"I should have known he would not keep the valuable gems where they might accidentally be found by his valet, unless he knows of the robberies," she muttered, tossing it aside.

She was lifting down a large box from a shelf in the armoire when a voice demanded, "Just what do you think you are doing?"

She whirled about, dropping the box to strike heavily upon her foot. Trevor was lounging in the doorway, watching her.

"I—that is—" She hopped about, favoring her injured foot as she sought for an explanation.

What might he do if he realized that she was looking for the plunder which she had already accused him of taking? Yet, what other reason could she give for her presence in his room?

Now that her first anger had cooled, she realized that she might be in danger from him. The man had bound and gagged Lady Foresham, who did not know who he was. He would know it was necessary to use more drastic measures to silence *her*, since there was no way to prevent her from knowing who he was.

"I see." He sounded as if she had made full explanation. Looking at the tangle of clothing upon the bed, he said, "Evidently, you feel that my valet does not have enough to do. I doubt he would agree. Nor would he approve of the state of my apparel. I fear he will be giving me his notice when he sees this."

Stepping within the room, he closed the door behind him. "But you need not have gone to so much trouble as this, my dear. I should have been more than happy to oblige, had I known what you wished."

"Wha—what do you mean?"

"Why, when a young female—even one who tries to lead the world to believe that she is not so young—comes into a man's bedchamber, it can only be for one of two reasons. And since you clearly did not come to bring fresh linens for my bed, I must assume—"

"You—you are insulting." First James had made such accusations about her; now Trevor was doing the same. But Trevor, at least, knew there was no truth in what he was saying.

Perhaps she could face him down and make her escape from the room, but she doubted she could do so; she did not like the way he was looking at her. Why had she not brought one of the footmen to protect her? No such thought had come to her earlier; she had been too angry at Trevor's behavior to think of anything else. She attempted to edge around him to the door, but he caught her arm and swung her to face him.

"Insulting? I think not." Before she could utter any further protest, he fastened one hand in her hair, casting her wig aside. His other arm was tight about her waist and his mouth came down to crush her lips brutally.

A well-bred lady should swoon at such treatment, Felicia thought wildly. If she swooned, however, it would not be from outrage, but because the feelings going through her had turned her knees to jelly while rockets seemed to be going off within her head. Every nerve seemed to carry the fiery message his lips were imprinting upon hers, until she felt she must burst into flame.

When he finally broke off the kiss, she felt as if she had been spun about in a whirligig. The hands she had put up in an attempt to push him away were scrabbling at the front of his waistcoat, as much to support herself as in an attempt to embrace him, while his lips left hers to wander about her face and throat.

She uttered a sound midway between a sigh and a moan as his teeth caught her earlobe, nipping it gently. His breath was warm, stirring her hair, as he whispered, "And shall I show you what else happens to little girls who come to a man's bedroom?"

"I—I—no—NO!" Tearing herself from his embrace, Felicia fled, her face scarlet, as the sound of his laughter followed her down the hall. The man was a scoundrel, a blackguard, a . . .

Inside her own room, she bolted the door, then leaned against it, her fist pressed against her mouth, less to banish the feeling his kiss had left upon them than to force down the emotions rising within her.

The man was a scoundrel, a blackguard, everything she should dislike—and she loved him!

# * Ten *

FOR HOURS, FELICIA alternately paced about her room or sank into a chair and stared into space, twisting her handkerchief into knots until the cloth shredded in her nervous fingers. What was she to do, how was she to solve this turmoil in her life? Nothing in her earlier days could have prepared her for this turnabout in her emotions.

There was no way that she could forgive herself for feeling as she did. She had always prided herself upon the coolness of her head. But, of course, her head had nothing to do with the way in which her heart was misbehaving.

She was unhappy enough now, knowing that she had lost that heart to a thief who preyed upon people to whom she had introduced him, but much worse could be in store for her. If Trevor were to be apprehended during one of his crimes, something that must certainly happen . . . As he had told her when she had first accused him of being a thief, she could be judged equally as guilty as he for having made it possible for him to meet these people and learn about their jewels.

Still, she knew that—except for how she would have ruined Holly's future if she were apprehended along with Trevor—she cared less about her own possible fate than about the punishment Trevor would face when he was caught. Could she, only a few hours ago, wished he could be tortured for his crimes? That must have been a different person from the one who was pacing about, worrying about the man's future. She was certain that, whatever he must undergo, she would suffer as much as he, even if she were not punished for helping him.

"I know that something dreadful is certain to happen if he keeps on stealing. He will be arrested, perhaps even killed while attempting to escape. But can I convince him that he should stop? If I go to him, begging him to be careful, will he only think I wish him to make love to me again?"

Great as her concern was for Trevor's safety, she did not dare approach him another time. When she remembered how eagerly she had responded to his kisses, she could feel her face burning with shame. How amused he must be to know he could rouse such feelings in her.

"I cannot face him, cannot bear to see how he will mock at me now. He had no *right* to make me fall in love with him." She said the words angrily, yet she knew that Trevor had done nothing to attract her; in fact, everything he had done since he had first walked into this house had been designed, it had seemed, with the purpose of stirring her to fury.

Even now, his kiss had been intended as a punishment, rather than an act of love. The remembrance of her own actions would have been bad enough if she thought he cared for her, but she knew he did not.

She was still in her bedchamber, attempting vainly to regain control of her emotions, when Holly returned from her shopping trip. Although she had purchased nothing, the girl appeared to be glowing with happiness. Felicia's attempts to greet her casually failed completely, and the younger girl looked at her in some alarm.

"What is it, Felicia? Are you ill?"

"No, not ill," Felicia hastened to reassure her. Holly

must not know what had happened during this tumultuous afternoon.

How could her sister be made to understand why James had accused *her* of improper behavior with Trevor? What was much worse would be attempting to explain about her own changed feelings about Trevor—something which Felicia herself did not understand.

"It is only that I am somewhat overtired. After all, we have been trotting very hard since we came to London. You seem to be taking to this running about better than I; I suppose it is because you are so much younger. I think I shall not come down to dinner this evening, since we have no plans to go out later."

"You do not wish to come to dinner? You must not feel well; I have never known you to ail for anything. Shall I ask to have our dinner brought up so that we can eat together?"

"No, do not do that. I am not ill, Holly. Truly I am not. It is only that I—I do not feel hungry tonight. You go down and join T-Trevor for dinner when you have changed."

Holly shook her head. "No. Hastings said that Trevor had left the house, saying he would not return until late. It will be lonesome eating by myself. Let me have dinner up here with you."

"So Trevor has gone out." She had thought he would stay to laugh at her when next they met for her behavior with him.

Automatically, Felicia straightened her wig, which had been pushed askew while she had paced about. Trevor had left it outside her door, another reminder of what had occurred in his bedchamber. She had angrily put it on, but wished she might throw it aside forever. Whenever she wore it now, she knew she would recall its being tossed away just before Trevor had kissed her.

For the moment, at least, she was spared the necessity of seeing him again. She knew that Holly was never entirely happy in her own company, but there was no need to have the servants bring the food up to them, merely so her sister could have someone near her while she ate.

"I suppose you have the right of it, Holly. I ought not to insist that you eat alone, simply because I am a bit fatigued. I shall change my gown and we shall have a comfortable little dinner, just the two of us, as we were used to do. Then, if you should wish to go out later, I am certain we can find something of interest in our many invitations."

Holly, however, was content to remain at home after they had dined. She complained that she, too, was overtired by the many balls and outings they had attended, and would like an early night.

For the present, Felicia had given over her plans for a ball for Holly. She still hoped to find a proper suitor for her, unless James Harrison told everyone what he suspected was taking place in the house at Grosvenor Square. If he did say anything, Holly's future was blasted, for no one would believe that she could be innocent if she lived beneath the same roof with a pair who were behaving in an improper manner.

However, he might be gentlemanly enough to wish to protect Holly, no matter what he thought of Felicia's behavior. No matter, the plans for the ball must wait until she learned what would happen.

To Felicia's relief, Trevor had gone out before she and Holly went down to breakfast. He would have to be faced sometime, but she was happy that she need not do so for the moment. Perhaps she would be calmer by the time they met again.

She had heard him come into the house long after midnight, less silently than he was in the habit of moving about, and hoped that he had not been committing another theft. True, the others had taken place only after the three of them had attended some affair, but there were other houses in which they had been guests, giving him the opportunity to look about and decide what he might take. For the remainder of my life, she told herself, I shall go in fear of what might befall him. It would not matter if she never saw him again; the fear for his safety would still be there.

In an attempt to conceal her worry about Trevor, she suggested to Holly that they ride in the Park again this morning. She was still hoping that James Harrison had not passed on the tale Trevor had told him, and that there was still the opportunity to find someone for Holly.

The younger girl was loath to go riding. "I promised Celia that I would go with her again today to visit the shops," she protested. "She will not understand if I say I preferred to go riding than to go with her, for she knows I do not care to ride."

"We shall go for an hour only," Felicia promised her. "That will certainly leave time enough for the two of you to go about your shopping. I notice that you did not bring home anything from yesterday's outing, although I expected you to be laden with gimcracks. Did Celia find many things she liked?"

"Oh, neither of us were truly interested in making purchases. It is much more exciting just to walk about and see what is in some of the shops, and wonder about the people who might purchase some of the things. It is more entertaining than visiting a play." At least, it had not been so difficult for her to understand as the play they had attended at the theater.

"I should never have thought you would get so much enjoyment from observing others." Holly had never shown any similar interest in the people at home. However, she had known them all her life and there could be nothing new about any of them to pique her interest. Watching the actions of people in London must be somewhat like seeing the animals in a menagerie. "Do not allow them to know you find them odd," she warned.

Holly's laugh contained a note of embarrassment, her sister thought. She was quick to explain, "Oh, we do not say anything except to each other, but it *is* exciting. Some of the gentlemen are so foppish that they are completely ridiculous—"

"I hope the two of you have not done anything so foolish as to go down St. James's Street," Felicia said in sudden alarm. "Surely, Celia's maid—"

"Oh, we should not do that. Mariette—"

"Who is Mariette?" Had they met some new friend about whom she knew nothing?

"She is Celia's maid, of course. And she had told us no lady would permit herself to be seen there, where the gentlemen sit, looking from the clubs. I do not know why they should do that, but perhaps it is something like the way we watch the shoppers. Do you suppose that is their reason, Felicia?"

"Oh, I suppose it might be something of the kind." She knew no more about what happened there than did Holly, but she had heard it was no place for a lady to go.

"We spend our time among the shops upon Bond Street, which is unexceptional—except for the people we see. You cannot imagine how some of them are dressed. And I know Celia will be disappointed if I do not come."

"I should dislike to have that happen, and it seems a simple enough pleasure. I think you may plan on going with her—after we have our ride."

"Then let us hurry with our ride. And you need not worry about me, even if Evans does not go with me. Celia's Mariette watches over us quite well, and does not mind that I go along. She says that the two of us are no more trouble than one will be."

"It sounds as if Mariette must have been with the family

for some time, if she speaks in such a manner about her mistress. None of our new servants would dare to speak in that way."

She recalled Evans's complaint about Holly's running in the street, but said nothing about it now. That was an unusual occasion and would never be repeated, for Holly would not again be so tempted. To mention that would be to remind Holly of Andrew Marsh—and that must not happen.

"Oh, Celia says she has been there forever. I think she was abigail to Celia's mother, and I know she was Celia's nurse when she was small."

"Then she can certainly be depended upon to watch both of you. But if you see something you wish to purchase, you must do so. There must be any number of interesting trinkets in the shops. Be certain that you take enough money with you for I should not wish you to borrow from Celia. And do not carry your parcels; have them sent home. Now, hurry and have Evans help you into your habit. It does us good to be seen in the Park, even at this early hour."

Felicia was pleased when they arrived home from their morning's ride. Two gentlemen, both quite eligible, asked permission to ride with them, squabbling amiably over which of them should be allowed to ride beside Holly whenever the path was not wide enough for all of them to ride abreast. Each of them apologized to Felicia, saying that they meant no discourtesy to her.

"But you know how it is, Miss Arsdale," young Edward Amesby felt impelled to explain their behavior. He was a fair young man apparently quite proud of his luxuriant moustache, for he kept smoothing it while he spoke. "At balls, everyone takes up so much of Miss Holly's time that those of us who are not good dancers seldom get a moment of her company. It is such a privilege to have the opportunity to meet her in this way, where we might talk with her, before so many of our friends are about."

"I understand perfectly, Mr. Amesby," Felicia told him with a laugh. "Young people prefer to talk to people of their own age, which is as it should be. And I like for Holly to have pleasant companions."

Neither Mr. Amesby nor his friend, Sir Kenneth Wray, could compare in family importance with James Harrison, but both were quite acceptable. If either of them should offer for Holly, her future would be settled—provided nothing went wrong, Felicia told herself, unwilling to put her fear into words. Still, the fear was there, lurking behind her thoughts, causing her to wonder if she would ever be able to ensure Holly's future. With the other worry about Trevor's danger, she had trouble concentrating on what the gentlemen were saying.

Nonetheless, she smiled and exchanged light conversation with Mr. Amesby, and later with his friend, Sir Kenneth who was as dark as his friend was fair, but at least was clean shaven. She was certain she had given no hint of her private worries. If the morning's conversation could be believed, it should not be a difficult task to bring either of Holly's admirers to the point of making an offer.

She gave both gentlemen permission to call upon the morrow, regretting that Holly had already made plans for this afternoon, and returned home, feeling that this might be a successful Season after all.

Unwilling to spend the afternoon alone, for she knew she would think of Trevor and did not wish to do so, she accompanied Holly to Lady Brompton's and turned her over to the company of Celia and the watchfulness of Mariette, while she and the old lady engaged in a long conversation about the *ton* in general and in particular.

Felicia felt more at ease with the old lady than with any of those who were of the age she was pretending to be. Somehow, she feared they might penetrate her disguise and she had found she had no interests in common with them, because much of their talk was their assignations.

Lady Brompton was full of gossip, much of it rather scandalous, but it was about people in high places. She had been acquainted with Mrs. Fitzherbert during her "marriage" with the Prince Regent, although she confessed to having lost contact with the lady in late years since the royal liaison had ended.

"To be frank, my dear, everyone thought that she was much more of a lady than that foreign princess he married," her ladyship confided. "But, of course, he could never have obtained the king's permission for a true marriage with Maria."

Felicia nodded. Mrs. Fitzherbert, she had learned, had been considered ineligible for several reasons, especially because of her religion.

"Of course, Prinny has had any number of mistresses since that time. Not that his affairs have been conducted in secret. Nor, for that matter, have the indiscretions of the Princess of Wales been kept quiet. That could scarcely have been possible, for any number of people have seen her in Italy with her latest gallant. Thank Heaven, young Princess Charlotte does not appear to wish to follow the example of either of her parents, but is planning a proper marriage. To have a reprobate for our king will be bad enough, but acceptable. We have had similar kings in the past, I believe. To have a queen of loose morals might well destroy the kingdom."

"I confess I do not know much about these matters," Felicia said. "Such talk seldom reached us before we came to London, and since that time, I have been concerned more with seeing that Holly's Season is successful than in taking note of the doings of royalty."

What things she had heard, she thought should be none of her concern. Nor should they be the concern of others, except, perhaps, as they might affect the government. She was careful not to say too much to Lady Brompton. The *ton* was always a hotbed of gossip, so why should her ladyship behave differently from any other?

"When you reach my age, which will be many years more, I am certain, you will find that there is not much one can do except to store up tales of the indiscretions of others."

"I should not say that." Felicia was forced to laugh at that. "I know of no one who is more active in society than you, my dear lady. Do you not attend almost every event that takes place?"

"I own that there are few evenings that I do not get about, except for tramping about in Vauxhall. That, I fear, would be too much for my old legs. Of course, I have Celia to chaperon to these affairs, but between the pair of us, that is frequently only an excuse, so that I may see what is going on in the *ton* this Season, as I have done for so many Seasons past."

"And will do so for many Seasons to come, I have no doubt," Felicia assured her, causing the old lady to break into a cackling laugh.

"Nor I—I wish too much to know what is going on in the world about me. And I cannot depend upon people to tell me what I wish to know, so it is best to go about and discover it for myself."

Despite Felicia's protests that she must take her leave when the prescribed time for calls had passed, Lady Brompton persuaded her to stay longer, declaring, "You know what I think of those rules, and I know of no one whom I should more like to have near me than you, my dear. Stay at least until some other callers come, and we can hope they do not."

That settled the matter and, as no other callers did arrive, the afternoon proceeded amiably, with Lady Brompton reciting more of the old scandals, beginning with ones about most of the royal dukes, whose misdeeds would have filled many volumes, it seemed. One had been accused of selling army commissions, another of incest and murder, while a third had ten—at latest count—love children.

"There is no rumor about them, of course. The duke lives quite openly with their mother and acknowledges them all. It is known that he would marry her, were it not for the Royal Marriage Act, forbidding any of them to marry without the consent of the king. That was the same act which caused the breakup of Prinny's relationship with Maria Fitzherbert. Although they did continue for some time after he wed Princess Caroline, he was not truly bound to Maria, so eventually found another. Although he may well have done so, even if he *had* been married to her."

After disposing of royalty, Lady Brompton continued down through various lesser members of the *ton*. She listed many of the indiscretions of some of the Patronesses of Almack's, especially Lady Jersey and Countess Lieven, both of them demanding such exemplary behavior from the young ladies who attended Almack's, while they gave them an entirely different example by their private lives.

Only the Cits were spared, Lady Brompton considering them unworthy of her notice. Felicia was sometimes shocked at the old lady's frankness, but nonetheless forced to laugh at some of the tales.

When Holly and Celia returned, she bade a reluctant farewell to the Lady Brompton and bore her sister home, noting again that neither of the girls had actually made any purchases. It appeared that Holly was correct in saying that their enjoyment was found merely in looking at the goods in the various shops and in watching the other shoppers.

Trevor was again absent from the dinner table that evening, and when Felicia met him at breakfast, he gave no indication of recalling anything about the scene in his bedchamber. There was not the slightest hint of mockery in his voice or his eyes.

Apparently he did not consider it worth remembering, Felicia told herself, uncertain whether to be happy or angry at this. Those brief moments which had completely changed her life had not disturbed him in the slightest. Doubtless, he was in the habit of caressing females whenever the opportunity arose. And he would have considered her appearance in his bedchamber as sufficient excuse for such behavior. Well, she assured herself, I shall see that no such future opportunity arises here.

For some reason she could not explain, the thought saddened her.

When Holly spoke of again spending the afternoon with Celia, Felicia reminded her that the two young gentlemen who had ridden with them yesterday were to call upon her this afternoon. Holly pouted, which Felicia could never recall her having done before when given a task, then went upstairs to write a message to Celia, explaining why she could not come.

Felicia looked at her, shaking her head. She had heartily approved of Holly's friendship with Celia, who was so much more sensible than many of the young ladies she had met during the Season, but she had not brought her sister to London to spend all her time in gazing into shops.

"I suppose," she said half-aloud, "I should be happy that she does not want to purchase every bit of ribbon and feather that she sees and come to look like one of the Armstrong trio. But it is time that she shows a preference for one of the gentlemen she has been meeting. I did not bring her to London to waste her time, but to find her a husband. Either of those gentlemen who are coming today would do quite well. Then, I could go home where I could forget Trevor—and everything that has happened since I came to London." Deep inside, however, she knew it would not be easy to forget him.

Mr. Amesby and Sir Kenneth arrived at the same moment, although, from the looks they exchanged, this was not by any design of theirs. Each of them bore a huge bouquet of delicately tinted flowers, quite suitable for a young lady. Forbearing to laugh at the barbed glances they exchanged, Felicia welcomed them, bade them to take seats, and told Hastings to have word sent up to Holly that her visitors were here.

"But Miss Holly has gone out, my—Miss," Hastings replied.

Would he never break himself of that habit of almost calling her "my lady," Felicia wondered, as she echoed, "Gone out?"

"Yes, m-Miss. Several hours ago. Lady Brompton's carriage arrived for her and she left at once. It was the same arrangement as in the day before yesterday, so I supposed that you were aware that she had gone."

"I cannot understand it. She knew—" She caught herself and said, "I must ask both of you to forgive my niece. It appears that she misunderstood the time of your arrival. I am certain that her friend has asked her to keep her company on some trivial errand and she will return soon."

She knew, however, that Holly had *not* misunderstood her instructions to remain at home and meet the visitors. The girl had deliberately disobeyed Felicia's orders, and had contrived to slip out of the house without her sister's notice.

Holly was usually so biddable that Felicia found herself wondering what there was about browsing through the shops that Holly found so irresistible. Could it be that the thought of marriage was beginning to frighten her? She had given no sign of such feelings—or had Felicia been too much involved in making her plans to notice what was happening to Holly?

The young gentlemen looked miserably at one another. To forget such a call was tantamount to giving one the cut direct; on the other hand, much could be forgiven to one who was so lovely as Miss Holly Arsdale.

"Perhaps it is we who are at fault," Sir Kenneth ventured. "We have come much too early. Shall we return later in the day? Miss Holly might enjoy a drive in the Park."

"Not likely; if she has already gone driving, she will not wish to go out again," his companion said. "It might be better if we planned to call upon her tomorrow, that is, if she has no plans."

"Oh, I am certain that she has not." Felicia was determined that Holly would be present when the gentlemen called again, even if she must lock the girl in her room until they arrived. Holly must not be permitted to behave in such a fashion; her entire future depended upon finding some proper husband for her. "I must apologize for the child; she had been so busy since we came to London that she doubtless confused her engagements."

"Quite understandable," Sir Kenneth said, although his tone implied that he did not understand at all how *he* could have been forgotten. Mr. Amesby did not speak, but Felicia was certain he felt much the same. How could Holly have been so—so inconsiderate, when she knew her future depended upon pleasing some gentleman?

"At least, they have promised to call again, so all is not lost," Felicia reassured herself, sinking into a chair as the door closed behind the pair. It was opened again almost at once, and Hastings came to announce, "Mr. James Harrison."

"I am no longer at home to Mr. Harrison, Hastings," Felicia told him, the memory of his words at their last meeting all too clear.

"Do not say that," the young man cried, brushing past Hastings. "I must speak to you."

"I believe everything was said at our last meeting. Hastings, will you please show Mr. Harrison to the door?"

Before Hastings could move to obey, James had closed the door in his face and turned to Felicia. "Please," he begged, "you must listen to me. Allow me to say how sorry I am for the scene I made the last time I was here. I wronged you beyond forgiveness, I know, by the things I said, but I am hoping that you will be kind to me."

Before Felicia could think of a scathing reply, he caught her hands, led her to the sofa, then sank to his knees at her feet.

She made a vain attempt to free her hands. "What do you mean, wronged me?"

"Perhaps that is not the right word, but still I say it. Since the moment I left here, I have thought again and again of what that fellow Thomas said to me. And I think he lied."

"It is something he does very well." Felicia thought of the many lies he had told her, of the many he had forced her to tell for him.

"However, it does not matter."

"Does not matter?" With a wrench, Felicia freed her hands from his grasp and rose. "How can you say it does not matter? If the creature has been telling lies about me, it matters a great deal."

"Of course it matters in that way. He should not be permitted to go about maligning you, and I hope to be able to do something about his behavior before much time has passed. But I mean that, even if what he said is true, I do not care. I do not care even that I saw him holding you in his arms. I care only about you."

"What you are saying makes no sense." In truth, she wondered if he realized the meaning of his words. Or the meaning she could impute to them if she wished. Was he truly ready to overlook the fact that she had been (as he thought) another man's mistress?

"To me, it makes a great deal of sense. What I am attempting to tell you is that, regardless of anything that might have occurred, I want you to be my wife. I may have said some cruel things to you—I know I did so. But it was because I had just come from talking with Thomas. When I had time to think clearly, I knew that nothing you could do would change my feelings for you."

"Please, James—" Felicia walked to the window and stood with her back to him. She bit her lip and attempted to keep tears from her eyes.

If only he had said those words to her before she realized that it was Trevor Thomas whom she loved. At the moment, she hated Trevor for making her love him, for making her unfit to accept any substitute.

Returning to face James, she said, "I am so sorry, my dear, but we just would not suit."

"Think about it, I beg of you—perhaps you will find that we should suit very well."

"No, the difference in our ages—"

"Makes no difference."

"More than that, I am not the person you think." She drew off her wig, smiling at his look of shock. "We are all masqueraders here, except for Holly. And Trevor was telling you the truth, he is not my nephew. I had never seen him before we came to London, and I am merely sponsoring him, as I am sponsoring Holly."

"I—see." He appeared half-dazed, whether from the revelation that she was probably younger than he, or from her admission that Trevor had told the truth about their relationship, or lack of it. He realized that she had said she was "sponsoring" the fellow, but had said nothing about her feelings for him.

Felicia took his hand. "You see how it is, James. We

should *not* suit. You had best look for someone from your own class. And I shall go home."

He nodded, still at a loss for words, and turned away. When he opened the door, Hastings was standing outside with several of the footmen. "I thought you might be in need of assistance, my—Miss," he said.

Felicia laughed. "Do not be foolish, Hastings. One does not throw a Harrison out the door," she told him. "Even if there were a reason, which there is not. Good-bye, James, and be happy."

"If I can do so," he said mournfully and walked away until his coachman reminded him that he had driven to the meeting.

When the door closed behind him, Felicia stood silent for several moments, wishing that she had not had to hurt him. At last, she turned to the respectfully loitering Hastings. Refraining with difficulty from giving him a setdown for his curiosity about her affairs, she said, "When Miss Holly returns, please tell her I wish to see her at once."

"But this message arrived from her while you were with Mr. Harrison," he replied, handing her the missive. "I thought it best to wait till he had gone before presenting it."

What could have happened to Holly? She hated to write a message of any kind. She thanked the butler absently and ripped open the note.

"Dere Felisha (Holly never could spell, her sister thought) I know now that the reason you kept hinting me away from Trevor is not because he wants an ar—a rich wife, but because you have a ten—tend—you love him yourself. That is what Andrew says and I am certin he is right.

"I have not told you, becas I knew you wud not like it, but Andrew came back to London. He has been here this past sennit and I have seen him whenever I could get away. That is why I did not want Evans to go out with me. She wud hav told you. Celia's maid did not care that I was seeing him. I know I would never be happy here in London, so Andrew is taking me home. He tells me I can stay with his pare—his mother and father until we can marry.

"Please do not hate me because I know you have had grand plans for me. But Andrew is right, I belong in the country with him, not in the city. I do love you and thank you for what you wanted for me even if it was not what I wanted. Holly."

Felicia reread the scrawled missive as if she hoped to find that her first reading was wrong. After all her plans for Holly, all she had done to find her a wealthy husband, one who would be worthy of her beauty. . . . She could have brought James to see that it was truly Holly he wanted, not herself. Or she could have encouraged one of the other gentlemen to make an offer. And now Andrew had overset all her plans.

Holly had always listened to him, but Felicia had hoped that removing the girl from his influence would show her that the world had so much more to offer her. How *dared* Andrew follow them to London and talk to Holly behind her back? Of course, if he told Holly she ought to go home with him, she would do so.

All her grand plans for Holly's future ruined by that young man. They might as well have never come to London. At least, she would never have met Trevor and fallen in love with him. Trevor—who was certain to be arrested, and doubtless hanged for his thefts!

Felicia, who had always prided herself on being able to meet any situation calmly, flung herself upon the sofa and burst into noisy sobs.

# * Eleven *

THE MOMENT HE entered the house, Trevor heard her and brushed aside Hastings, who had been hovering beside the door, ready to announce him, and who doubtless was preparing to listen to what was about to be said. "Never mind that foolishness, you bufflehead," he told the man angrily. "I live here."

He closed the door tightly against Hastings's curiosity, then threw himself down beside Felicia and drew her to his chest. With a large handkerchief, he mopped her tear-stained face, murmuring, "Do not be in such a taking. Nothing can be so bad as that."

"It is much, much worse," she moaned, not wondering why he happened to be there, where she wanted him to be, but burying her face against the roughness of his coat. "You cannot know—"

Trevor removed the crumpled paper from her fingers and had managed to decipher the greater part of Holly's scrawl before Felicia remembered what Holly had written about *her* feelings for Trevor, and snatched it back from him. It was the truth, but he must not know.

"After—after everything I have done for Holly, to ensure her future, she does *this*—"

"They cannot have been gone long," he reassured her,

using his finger to wipe away the last of the tears. "Not more than an hour or so, I should think. If you wish, we can go after them. We should catch up to them before nightfall."

"No, if Andrew has taken her to his home, as I am certain he would have done, for he is much too proper to do anything else, they would already have arrived there before we could come up with them. And it would be a scandal if I descended upon them, demanding that she come back to London with me."

"Then you do not think they would have started for the border?" He stroked her hair, wondering that she was no longer wearing her wig, but was pleased to see how much prettier she was without it. Or would have been, if her eyes had not been red and swollen with weeping. The only other time he had seen her without it, he had been in no mood to look at her closely. On the other hand, he had been much too close to her to see her properly.

"Oh, there would be nothing of that kind, I am sure. Holly says that she is to stay with his parents until they are married, and I am certain that is what will happen. Andrew is doing her thinking for her now, and apparently has been doing so for some time, so she will do as he wishes. It was surely his idea for her to deceive me day after day with her tales of shopping excursions, for I cannot imagine she would be so untruthful to me without his urging. But I had such wonderful plans for her—and now, everything is ruined."

She appeared about to give way to her grief once more, so Trevor said quickly, "I think it is time, my girl—long past time, in fact—that you stopped thinking so much of Holly's future and began to give a bit more thought to your own."

"But—"

His mouth came savagely down upon hers, choking off

any further protest. For an instant, Felicia stiffened in his embrace, thinking of the last time he had kissed her. Then, knowing that this caress was far different from the last, despite its fierceness, she clung to him, returning his kiss with a passion that surprised her, but appeared to please him very much.

When at last his lips released hers, he smiled down at her. "That is what I mean, my dearest one. For all her dimness in other ways, your Holly had the right of this. I believe you love me as much as I love you."

"Oh, I do. I have done. For so long, although I did not know it for a time." All pretense put aside, Felicia knew she was committed to him, no matter what befell the two of them. "But you should go away, my dear one, go quickly— leave London. Every day you linger here, you are in more danger. And I do not know if I can bear to go on fearing for your safety. If you wish, I am willing to go wherever you like. It will not matter where it is, as long as you are there."

"But why should you think I should go anywhere?" His puzzlement appeared to be genuine. "I could understand if you thought it would be improper for me to remain in the house now that Holly has gone. But dangerous?"

"But that—"

"I could stay elsewhere—for the present. However, much as it pleases me to hear you say you are willing to go wherever I go, I have no wish to leave London before the end of the Season. It will be a much more enjoyable time for the both of us, now that we need no longer pretend about our feelings."

"You know why you should go." Why must he be so dense? "The jewels—"

"What jewels?"

"The stolen ones, of course. How long do you think you can go on before someone realizes—"

Trevor began to chuckle. "Is *that* what you were doing in

my bedchamber the other day? I thought it was merely some pique that made you throw my clothing about in such a fashion. And I assure you, my love, I *was* hard put to persuade my valet not to leave me, when he saw what had happened. It was not what he was accustomed to, he told me."

Felicia managed a weak laugh, remembering that Evans had said much the same thing about Holly's running in the street, then was serious again, remembering that was on the occasion of Andrew Marsh's first appearance in London, the beginning of Holly's disobedience of her wishes. However, her anger at Trevor at the time she ransacked his room was a far different matter. "Well, I must own that I was angry at you for what you had said to James—"

"Now, truly, my dear, you did not want the man, did you? He told me that he was planning to offer for you, and I was in a taking lest you might accept him, so I made up a tale to frighten him away. If you could not land him for Holly, you might feel that, as your husband, he could help you to find her a suitable match."

Felicia leaned back in his arms so that she could look into his face. "I do not understand it. Can you always read me so clearly as this?"

"Not all of the time, which I feel may be just as well, as I know there have been many occasions when you would gladly have thrown me to the lions. But if I have learned anything about you during the time we have been together, it is that you would stop at nothing to further Holly's cause. Even if it meant you must agree to marry a man you did not love."

"That is true, I did think I would do it. To help Holly."

"Only for that and not for what he could do for you? After all, he is a wealthy man." Was there an edge of jealousy in his tone, or had she imagined it? She thrilled to the possibility that she could make him jealous.

"No—truly." She reached up to stroke his face, aware that she had been wanting to do this for some time. "For all his money, there was nothing he could do for me, that I should have wanted, except to aid Holly. I felt that I could, if I must, agree to take him for that, and for no other reason."

"Yes, I thought you might feel that way." He captured her hand and held it against his cheek. The feel of the faint stubble against her palm sent a thrill through her. "But I am happy you did not find it necessary to go to such extremes."

She nestled against him once more, feeling safe for the first time in all the years since she had first become responsible for Holly. Safe, despite the danger that threatened Trevor, and therefore threatened her, as well.

"Yes, I would have done so. Just for her benefit. And see how she rewards me for all my pains. Running off with Andrew. And she must have been seeing him day after day, here in London. I know she met him one time, but she said he had to return home the next day. She did not mention that he had come to the city another time."

"Probably because she knew you would discourage her from seeing him. That is what he seems to think. Would you not have done so?"

She nodded. "If I had not thought her above Andrew's touch, I should not have brought her to London in the first place."

"Nor gone about in clothing more suited to someone's middle-aged aunt than to yourself. And wearing a gray wig. Where is your wig, by the way? Although I much prefer you without it."

"I forgot about it." She put her hand to her head. "It must be somewhere about. I remember that I took it off when I was telling James that I *had* been deceiving him all the time. Although not in the way you had given him to think."

"You told him that today?" Trevor sat up straighter.

"You mean he came to call on you again? I did not succeed in frightening him off?"

"Yes, you did so—at first. He came here to accuse me of—of . . . It was quite an unpleasant scene. But he returned today to tell me that it made no difference to him if you and I had been—had been—" She could feel her color rising and buried her face against his shoulder.

He caught a strand of her hair about his finger as he had done several times in the past. This time, however, she knew it was not done in mockery.

"My love, I did not say what I did to him in order to insult you, whatever you may think. However, I must own that I did wish to give Harrison the impression that you were mine. Perhaps I expressed myself more fervently than I planned, so that he gained an erroneous idea of our relationship."

"He had certainly done that. Yet he was so contrite in his apology today that I could not help feeling sorry for him."

"Not to the point of accepting him, I hope."

"No—never that. Not now. Although I *had* thought at one time that he would make an acceptable husband—for what he might help me to do for Holly. But that was before—before I knew—" Even now, she was hesitant to put into words how desperately she had come to love him.

"I am happy about that." Trevor drew her again into the tight circle of his embrace and the words were murmured against her lips. "I should not wish for you to be labeled a jilt."

"No—if I had promised, I must have kept my word. But even though you were not here, you would not permit me to agree."

Trevor rewarded this admission in a manner pleasing to both of them, and Felicia nestled happily in his embrace. She no longer worried about Holly's future. That was

Andrew's concern now; her own future lay with Trevor and she was content to have it that way.

There was a noise, almost a sound of scuffling in the hallway, and Lady Brompton's voice exclaimed, "Of course she is in no mood to see anyone, you nincompoop. I am fully aware of that. That is why I have come."

Hastings was unwilling to lay hands upon her ladyship and before he could think of any other way of forestalling her, she had opened the door to the drawing room and stepped inside, Celia at her heels. At the sound of her voice, Felicia had struggled to free herself from Trevor's arms, but he was reluctant to let her go, so that Lady Brompton could see in an instant what had been occurring.

"Hm—I thought as much. Your nephew, eh?" She did not appear at all surprised by the sight. Nor was she displeased.

It was Celia who cried, "But your hair! Miss Arsdale, what has happened?" She could see that Miss Arsdale had been weeping, and hoped it had not been because of Holly. If it had been for that, Grandmama would give her another scold.

"That should be obvious, child. One hears of people whose hair has turned white overnight, but never of the opposite taking place, so one must presume a wig. I had thought as much, some time ago, but did not suspect the reason."

"Well, yes, it was a wig." Felicia had at last managed to draw herself out of Trevor's arms. "It is rather a long story, I must own, your ladyship."

"And one that is neither here nor there at the moment, I am certain. Or perhaps it is, at that. I have been able to persuade my granddaughter to confess the part that she and that ungrateful creature Mariette have played in your niece's—?"

"My sister's."

Trevor raised his eyebrows at the admission. "I had supposed that she was only a friend you had agreed to sponsor."

"I had not thought that, but you did not seem to be a proper aunt. But now that I can see how young you are, it explains a great many things," Lady Brompton said with a satisfied nod. "The added years were meant to be a safeguard against gossip, I suppose."

Felicia nodded. There seemed to be no more reason for keeping her masquerade a secret, now that Holly was gone. "We had no wish to employ some older lady to act as our chaperon, when I could do the task just as well. We could save a great deal of expense in this way. After all, it was only Holly for whom we needed to find a husband, and I could not be certain another lady would do as I wished in the matter."

"I can understand you had not planned for *this*." She exchanged almost conspiratorial glances with Trevor. "I feel, however, that an older lady might have been more strict with the girl. Still, she may have managed to pull the wool over another's eyes, as well as she must have done over yours. As I was about to say when we first arrived, Celia has confessed to me that she and Mariette have been making it possible, with their fiction of shopping trips, for Holly to meet with that young man."

"We meant no harm to anyone," Celia said tearfully. "It was only that Holly was so much in love—"

"Rubbish! How can a child of that age know what love is?"

"It has been difficult even for ones not so young to recognize the emotion," Trevor commented, earning himself a glare from Felicia.

"I do not know if Holly truly loves Andrew—"

"Oh, she does. Mariette says—"

"That is another thing," her ladyship said sternly. "I

should have packed Mariette off without her notice over her part in this, but she has been with the family since the beginning of time. Or so it seems. But to aid in an elopement—"

"It is not so bad as it sounds," Trevor told her. "Felicia is certain that Holly is going to the young man's parents."

"But you do not approve of her choice," her ladyship said to Felicia.

"I do not suppose it matters now whether I do or not," she said with a deep sigh. "I know that Holly has had a long acquaintance with Andrew, and appears to prefer him to any of the gentlemen she has met since we came to London. And she has always been willing to do whatever he thinks she should do. Therefore, I have no choice but to allow her to wed him. Since I shall be returning home soon, it does not matter."

"That is something we have not yet settled," Trevor told her, again wrapping a strand of hair about his finger, as if he had forgot they were not alone. "I mean the matter of your leaving London."

"Oh, but we must. You know that. And you would be safe in my home; no one would think to search for you there."

"Oh, that." Trevor began to laugh. "Lady Brompton, will you—"

At that moment, both of them realized how remiss they had been and were on their feet. "Lady Brompton, we are being inexcusably rude," Felicia exclaimed. "Will you not have a seat? And let us have some tea sent in."

Trevor was bringing forward chairs for her ladyship and Celia. The old lady chuckled as she sat down.

"I should say the pair of you had other matters on your minds than tea."

"Well, you might say that we have," Trevor told her with

another laugh. "But will you please tell this foolish girl that I did *not* steal your necklace?"

"Trevor!"

"That is what is worrying you, is it not?" he asked reasonably.

"Oh, I have never thought that you could be the one," Lady Brompton assured him. "However, I do not doubt that you would make a success of such a theft if it should occur to you to attempt it."

"That is what I mean," Felicia protested. "Each time there has been a theft, it has been in a house where we have just attended some affair. What else am I to think but that you were responsible?"

"True, we were there—along with at least half of London. But I do not see why you should think that it was I, rather than another."

"For one thing," she protested, "you openly admired the daring of the thief. You could slip in and out of the house so easily. I knew that from the way you first arrived in my home. And I could not think of any other reason for your being so eager to attend those affairs. Except at first, of course, when I thought you were going in search of a wealthy wife."

"I did have another reason—several of them. But at least, you have acquitted me of the charge of wishing to marry for money. Have you not?"

"You know that I have."

Lady Brompton chuckled, recalling them to the fact that they were no longer alone. Felicia sank into a chair, her hands over her face, while Trevor, apparently unperturbed by having his romance observed by the old lady, stepped to the door and asked Hastings, who was still lingering in the hallway, beset with curiosity, to have tea sent in.

"What makes you think that the young man is the guilty party, Felicia?" Lady Brompton asked. Celia was staring from one to the other of them, wide-eyed. She would have liked to ask a number of questions, but thought it best not to call more attention to herself, lest she again be blamed for helping Holly to elope.

"Aside from admiring the thief, there was an occasion when I accused Trevor of having been responsible for the thefts—and he owned to having done it."

"Not truly," he protested. "I merely said it would be a good way of getting money if one needed it."

He sounded as if he was telling the truth, but Felicia did not believe him. He had frequently sounded innocent in the past, when she knew he had been nothing of the sort. However, it mattered not at all to her what he had done, if only she could persuade him that he must go away from London before he was caught. If she went with him, she thought she could persuade him not to steal again.

"What has happened in the past does not matter now," Lady Brompton said. "If the pair of you can stop your bickering for a moment, I wish to beg your help."

"Certainly—how may we help you?"

"I am giving a dinner party this evening. I know the notice is short, that is why I am delivering the invitations in person." She did not appear to realize that all her invitations to them had been equally abrupt.

"But I cannot come out in public," Felicia protested. "Not now. Holly—"

"We can tell everyone that Holly has become so fatigued from the press of invitations that she has taken to her bed. You would have stayed with her, but have attended to please me."

"I suppose I might do that, if you think I should, but people will think it odd that I left her."

"Certainly not, they will find nothing odd about it; they will think you are merely being kind to an old lady by giving me your company. However, I think it might be best if you resumed your wig for the evening. I intend to give my guests enough of a shock, as it is."

"You are planning something, are you not?" Trevor hazarded, looking at her sharply.

"Yes—this is to be a farewell party for my jewels. I know I have talked bravely about what I should do if I saw the thief, but I do not feel nearly so brave as that, if the truth were told. On the morrow, I intend to gather up all my jewels—the necklace I have been wearing since the theft, my rings, bracelets, even my tiara. Everything is going to Rundell and Bridge, to be put in their safe until this villain has been caught."

"But if you fear the thief might strike again, would it not be wiser for you to say nothing about what you plan to do?" Felicia asked. Trevor, I pray you will not do this, she begged silently. Not to her.

"No, I want the word to be spread about that I shall no longer have anything in my house worth the taking. I can consider myself fortunate that he took only the one necklace the first time. Although its loss meant much to me for sentimental reasons, the jewels I still have are worth a great deal more, and I do not wish to lose them."

"I hope you are not making a mistake in telling this to everyone," Trevor observed, grinning at Felicia when the old lady was not looking.

"Never fear, young man. I know what I am doing. This way, I know that my jewels will be safe."

With only a bit more talk, she went on her way, saying that she had more invitations to deliver. Celia followed her, happy that nothing more had been said about her having abetted Holly. She doubted that she would truly be let off so easily, but at least at the moment, Grandmama had other things on her mind. And since Miss Felicia did not appear to mind that Holly had gone . . .

Why had she been wearing a gray wig all this time, and

why discard it now? Was it true that Trevor was not the lady's nephew, after all, but something far different? There was something happening at the house today that she did not fully understand.

Felicia was reluctant to attend Lady Brompton's dinner for several reasons. She had not been able to reconcile herself to Holly's elopement, although she told herself she had no choice but to do so. Also, she was in great fear that her ladyship was making an error in displaying all her jewels and speaking of her plans for removing them from danger. Doubtless, the servants in every house where she had left one of her invitations knew of her plan—and everyone knew how servants would gossip.

"Still," she told herself as she emerged from Miller's hands arrayed for the evening, "that might be a good thing. I pray Trevor will not attempt the theft, but if he does so, the fact that such a great number of people have known of Lady Brompton's plans will prevent anyone from suspecting him."

Why, she asked herself, did she have to love a thief? She would forever be wondering when he would be apprehended and face the hangman's rope. What happiness could there be for her, unless she could persuade him to give up his schemes and go away with her?

At the head of her dinner table, Lady Brompton was literally aglitter with diamonds. Below what Trevor had called her "second-best" necklace, more than a half-dozen brooches of various sizes were pinned across her bosom. She wore all her rings, several bracelets, and the tiara crowned her gray head.

At any other time, so great a display of wealth would have been considered quite vulgar, even for one who was accustomed to wearing great amounts of it, but Lady Brompton's diners stared at the jewels, hearing again what most of them must have heard more than once during the day—that this was the last time any of them would see her diamonds until the jewel thief had been apprehended.

Despite the brevity of the notice, there were forty people gathered about her large table, and Felicia could not help pitying the servants who had been forced to prepare for so many diners with no warning. Doubtless, her ladyship's chef was in the habit of preparing great meals quickly, for, in addition to customary roast beef and mutton, there appeared on the long table a jugged hare, a turkey, several soups, vegetables from boiled potatoes to fresh asparagus, mushrooms and spiced carrots, as well as several kinds of bread. A floating island, three cakes, some meringues, and several baskets of sweetmeats had been provided for those whose tastes ran to such foods.

There were many inquiries as to Holly's absence from the dinner, and she repeated the tale of the girl's fatigue from the bustle of the Season. Holly was not ill, she said again and again; it was merely that she felt the child was in need of rest, so had prevailed upon her not to attend tonight's dinner. When the matter had been fully explained, Lady Brompton had been willing to excuse her.

There were many expressions of disappointment at Holly's absence from the dinner. Those of the young gentlemen were clearly sincere, those of less-favored misses and their mamas held more than a hint of satisfaction at not seeing her.

Felicia asked herself if her lies were worth the trouble. Everyone would know soon that Holly had gone home—home to marry an apothecary's assistant, when she might have had her choice of many important young men. She would not tell the true tale tonight, however, lest she spoil Lady Brompton's dinner.

Each time she looked away from one questioner or another, Felicia saw James Harrison's reproachful face across the table. She tried to ignore it, telling herself that she ought to be more insulted by his offer of overlooking her misstep than by the anger he had displayed when Trevor had first implied it.

When the dinner was ended and the reluctant guests began to depart, Lady Brompton put a hand on Felicia's arm. "Stay with me," she begged. "Allow everyone to think you are leaving, but have Trevor take the carriage without you. I shall need your help."

Wondering what the old lady had in mind, Felicia nodded and spoke to Trevor, telling him what her ladyship had said. He did not appear to be surprised, merely said, "Have word sent to me if you wish me to return the carriage for you later."

"I do not think it will be necessary for you to do that; I believe she wishes me to stay the night, and doubtless you have plans of your own."

"Nothing that I should not forget at once if you sent me word." The warmth in his tone brought the blood to her face, but she merely shook her head.

"No—do what you wish. I shall remain here. For some reason, her ladyship seems to feel that my company will be of help to her. I think she is beginning to repent having said what she did about the jewels." Would he be warned away, she wondered.

Several hours later, she sat rigidly in a chair in Lady Brompton's bedchamber, her mind going over and over what her ladyship had confided when they were alone.

"I know how the word must have gone around the city that my jewels would be out of reach tomorrow, so I think that the thief will come for them tonight. I want you beside me, to help apprehend him. Several of the footmen will be waiting to hear us and will rush in, so there will be nothing to fear. I only wish a witness to what is happening."

Oh, Trevor, Felicia begged silently, while she agreed to Lady Brompton's suggestion, please be wise enough to see

that she is laying a trap for you. Do not walk into it, I beg
of you, my love.

She wondered how Lady Brompton could sleep so easily
if she truly expected a visit from the thief, but the regular
snores from the center of the huge bed told that the old lady,
at least, had no worries about what might happen.

The clock on some far-off church tower tolled the hour of
one, then two. Certainly, it must have been longer than that
since the two had retired for the night. Every minute
dragged as if weighted with lead, while Felicia was hard put
to sit quietly beside the bed, wishing that morning would
show her that she had worried in vain.

There was a breeze from a suddenly opened window, the
faintest glimmer of a hooded lantern as a figure stole across
the room. Without a break in her "snoring" Lady Brompton
put out a hand and caught Felicia's, warning her to be still.

Instead, the younger woman sprang from her chair and
threw herself across the room, clutching the figure who had
his hands upon the jewels. "You must flee while you can,
my dear one," she cried. "Did you not know it would be a
trap?"

"I think I must resent your using endearments to anyone
but myself." There was no mistaking Trevor's voice, but it
came not from the figure she was grasping, but from the
doorway of the dressing room, where he appeared, carrying
a large candelabra. At the same time, two footmen, summoned by her ladyship's hand on the bell pull, rushed in
from their place in the hall.

Felicia gaped at Trevor, then at the man she held, aware
that, even in the dark, she should have known that *he* could
not be Trevor. This man was slimmer and not quite so tall.

"You—," she began to Trevor. "Then who—"

"Shall we see?" He came across the room, setting the
light upon the dressing table. He reached out a hand toward

the mask, but the other drew back, putting up his own hand to uncover his face.

"I suppose I knew you were setting a trap," James Harrison said, "but the lure of all those gems—the daring of taking them at the last possible moment—it was beyond resisting."

# * Twelve *

"OH, JAMES." FULLY clothed, Lady Brompton slipped from her bed and came to the culprit's side. "Why you, of all people, to become a thief? Certainly, you were not in need of money. If so, you had only to apply to me or another of your friends—"

"The money had nothing to do with it, Lady Brompton." His tone was suddenly full of anger. "But can you, or anyone, imagine how boring a life I have been leading for the past several years?"

"But your family—"

"Yes, my family. You may talk about them. Gerald, at least, has the title and the property to look forward to—but I have nothing. Never allowed to take any part in managing the estate; not even one of the smaller farms. Oh, they permit me to have plenty of money, as you say, my lady—I have always been given my share of that—but nothing to do except to make the same round of balls and parties, meeting the same people each year."

"But you have always appeared to enjoy your Seasons."

"As you say, but appearances are not all. I have had nothing to do, and that is boring indeed. It is not even necessary for me to ensure the succession; Gerald has done that, as well. I care nothing for the usual sports and have found there is no lure for me in gambling, when I can easily afford my losses. To stake my ability and my wits against the risk of being taken—this has been the greater gamble."

Lady Brompton placed her arms about him. "My dear boy, surely there was something better you might have done. If you had asked your father to allow you to help with the estate—"

"No, I tried that, but he merely laughed at me and told me not to worry him, that there was nothing that could not be done better without my interference. I have found only one thing I wanted, but that was denied me." He cast a reproachful glance at Felicia, which made her want to weep. "But this held some excitement for me, the chance to prove that I could get away unscathed each time. As I say, it has been a gamble. And I have lost the final throw. It had to happen sometime. I wonder what the old gentleman will say at the thought that his least favored son is to meet the hangman."

"Nonsense! You know that will not happen. Cranston would never permit it. And he has the power to prevent it. But I fear you cannot remain in London. The scandal, when everyone learns—"

"Quite right, my lady. I do have enough respect for the family name not to drag it in the mud, now that I have failed. It will have to be Canada or Jamaica—and, of the two, I think I should prefer to go to Canada. The climate would be more suitable. Jamaica will tend to make me lazy, I fear. If I am gone, there will be no scandal—or at least, not so much."

He caught Felicia's hand and drew it to his lips. "You are grieving for me, my dear, because you could not give me what I wished. You must not. This has been the most enjoyable Season I have spent in London, except for your refusal. Lady Brompton, if you will send a servant to my lodgings, the jewels will be given to him. I presume I may go now."

"Certainly, my dear," Lady Brompton said, tears streaming down her face. Trevor gave her his handkerchief and she nodded her thanks. James raised her hand to his lips, waved a farewell to Felicia and walked away, his shoulders straighter than she could recall having seen them. It was as if he were thinking fondly of the chances he had taken and won.

Until now.

Felicia felt some sympathy for him, but reflected that, while an earl's son might walk out the door after being caught in a theft, a man of lesser rank would have faced the gibbet—with no powerful father to see that it did not happen. It was the fate she had feared for Trevor since she had begun to suspect him. "Is he to go free, then?" she asked. "What is to prevent him from taking the jewels and running away?"

"Not James Harrison," Lady Brompton said. "You do not know him well, if you think that. As he said, he doubtless only became a thief to while away the time. He saw it as a different type of sport."

"Sport!"

"Yes, it was as wrong of him to do so as it would have been of any other man—worse, in fact, because he did not steal out of need. But he never truly wanted the jewels, only the gamble. He will do as he said, return them and leave the country."

"Doubtless to travel abroad in luxury." She knew she sounded bitter, but it was the thought that she had been mistaken in him, blaming Trevor for what James had done, which made her so.

"Not in luxury, I should think. Cranston will not be pleased when he learns what James has done. James was right when he said he was not the favorite. His father will pay his passage, I am certain, thankful to have him away without any scandal. And perhaps give him a small allowance. But barely enough to permit him to survive. He will have to earn his living—and I do not doubt it will be the making of him."

"It seems a small punishment for causing so much trouble."

"He did little harm, after all," Trevor commented. "No one was injured by what he did—and I still admire his daring."

"You would do so!"

"No, my dear, Trevor has the right of it. James made several of us unhappy for a time by his thefts, but we shall have our gems again. And he harmed no one, except for binding and gagging Lady Foresham. Which did her no real harm. I wish I had seen that."

Lady Brompton chuckled, then yawned. "It has been a long night, waiting to see who would come."

"Waiting! You were asleep," Felicia accused.

Her ladyship chuckled again. "Asleep? Not for one moment. I would not have missed taking a part in this for my other diamond necklace, although I sorry that it was James we caught. I should never have suspected him. If my snoring gulled you into thinking me asleep, you can see how it would have gammoned James."

Trevor laughed and raised her hand to his lips, his gesture as gallant as James's had been. "Lady Brompton, I salute you. The poor fellow had no chance at all against you."

"One has not lived as long as I without learning a thing or two, my boy. But now, take your lady home; I am anxious for my bed. And this time, with no thief to worry about, I mean to sleep."

When the front door closed behind them and Trevor whistled until William awoke to guide the carriage out of the alley where he had concealed it, Felicia said accusingly,

"How did it happen that you were there? Lady Brompton told me to send you home."

"I know she did so. But she also had a moment to speak to me, telling me to leave, then to come back secretly and hide myself where I would be close at hand in case of need. She did not think the thief would offer violence, but there was always the chance that it would happen."

"She told me the footmen would be waiting for her summons—and they were."

"But they might not have arrived in time. And it would have been you who was in danger, should he have turned angry at being taken. So I was ordered to be there, to be certain you were safe, as I should have been, without the order, when I suspected what her ladyship had in mind. You must imagine my feelings when I heard you addressing the thief in such loving tones—and urging him to flee."

"You know I thought it would be you!"

"I know that you did so." In the darkness of the carriage, he had slipped an arm about her, and now she could feel the chuckle he was attempting to suppress. "I have wondered why you always attributed the basest of reasons for my actions."

Her curiosity still unsatisfied, Felicia tried to draw away, but he held her close. "If I thought that," she complained, "it was because you gave me good reason. From the day we met, when you blackmailed me into calling you my nephew—"

"And how you disliked that, Auntie, my darling Auntie. But it was the only way I could be certain that I would know what you were doing."

"I never had any idea but to launch Holly in the *ton* and gain her a good husband."

"I know that now. But not at the first. You might well have been an imposter intending to take in some member of the *ton*."

"And I first thought you wanted to win a wealthy wife. After the thefts started, it seemed that they always took place where we had visited—"

"Along with at least half the *ton*."

"Well, I could think of no other reason for you to remain underfoot."

"Could you not? I could think of one very good reason." His lips sought hers. "I think I wanted to do that from about the second day I knew you."

"Then why should you go through all the pretense about unmasking me? And when I told you I was not Lady Felicia, you were not surprised to hear it. In fact, you told me at once that you could prove I was not she. How could you do so?"

"Easily, my dear one. You see, *I* have never made any attempt to deceive the *ton*. Lady Felicia Arsdale is truly my aunt. She does not interest herself in affairs of the London crowd, but I had heard there was a Felicia Arsdale taking a part in the Season."

She stared up at him, trying to read his features in the faint light of torches they were passing. "And," he continued, "I thought it my duty to discover exactly what the false Lady Felicia was doing in London. After all, you did not try too hard to convince people that you were not her ladyship, did you?"

"I suppose I did not," she owned. "It made it easier for me to obtain the invitations which I needed for Holly. Or which I thought I needed, which was the same thing. When I think of the time I wasted in trying to find her a proper husband—"

"Instead of allowing Nature to take its course. But do you truly think your London Season was wasted? For I do not. I clearly recall your saying that you would go with me anywhere I chose."

"That was before I discovered who you truly are. You cannot—"

"Cannot what?"

"Cannot expect the *ton* to accept me when they know I am an imposter."

"Do you think anyone will know that my young, lovely, brown-haired wife is the gray-haired maiden lady who was here for this Season? If they see a resemblance, we shall merely say that there is a distant relationship—as there is. People actually pay little attention to the appearance of others, except to what they are wearing, so I doubt the resemblance will be noticed. Too, I expect that we may wish to travel much of the time, not to save myself from the authorities, as you thought, but because we enjoy it, and will visit London only for the Season."

"I do not think—"

"Do not. Let me convince you that I know what is best."

Felicia struggled briefly, unwilling to permit even this dear man to make decisions for her—then relaxed in his arms, since he was deciding exactly as she wished him to do.

# Elane Osborn

# Skylark

*Hannah Bradley*: A glorious beauty who
loves hot air ballooning and traveling in
circuses.

*Quinton Blackthorne*: A dashing, but arrogant
nobleman who dwells in the finest circles of
London society.

It has been arranged for Quinton and Hannah to marry
others, but theirs is a love that cannot be denied. So the
two ignore their parent's marital plans and get swept up in
Hannah's life of ballooning and derring-do. But soon they
find themselves entangled with thieves and kidnappers.
Only the most powerful love will get them through this
adventure so they can follow their lifelong destiny.

___SKYLARK  (On sale Nov. 1990)  1-55773-410-0/$4.50

From the *New York Times* bestselling author
of <u>Morning Glory</u> and <u>Bitter Sweet</u>

# LaVyrle Spencer

One of today's best-loved authors of bittersweet
human drama and captivating romance.

| | |
|---|---|
| ___SPRING FANCY | 0-515-10122-2/$3.95 |
| ___YEARS | 0-515-08489-1/$4.95 |
| ___SEPARATE BEDS | 0-515-09037-9/$4.95 |
| ___HUMMINGBIRD | 0-515-09160-X/$4.95 |
| ___A HEART SPEAKS | 0-515-09039-5/$4.95 |
| ___THE GAMBLE | 0-515-08901-X/$4.95 |
| ___VOWS | 0-515-09477-3/$4.95 |
| ___THE HELLION | 0-515-09951-1/$4.50 |
| ___TWICE LOVED | 0-515-09065-4/$4.95 |
| ___MORNING GLORY | 0-515-10263-6/$4.95 |